UNHOLY WHISPERS OF SAINT AMBROSE

KEITH MCDUFFEE

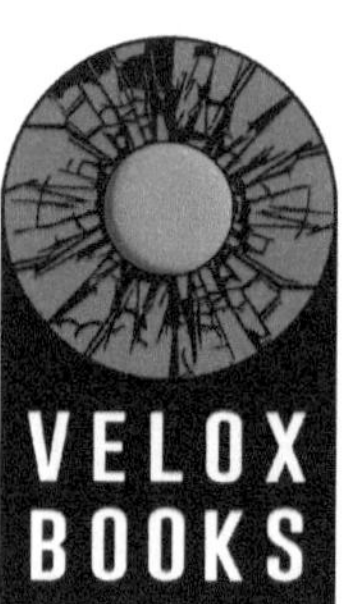
VELOX
BOOKS

**FOLLOW VELOX TO KEEP
THE NIGHTMARES COMING:**

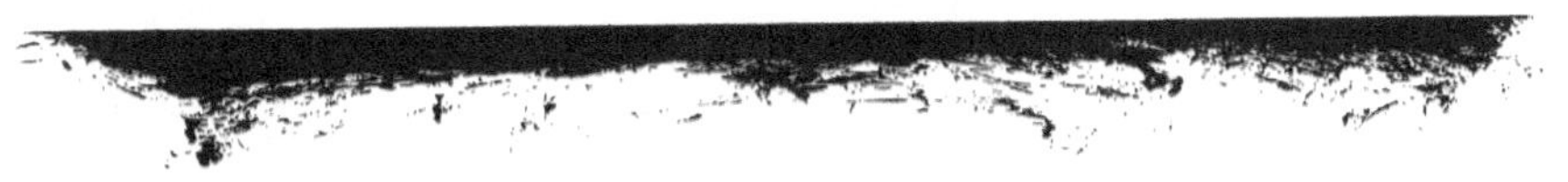

CONTENTS

A NOTE FROM THE CARETAKER

Well, you've found me, haven't you? Yes, for me, at least during what may be a brief stint as head decon here, it is home. The same cannot be said of most others here. Saint Ambrose, a place of eternal rest, solemn reflection, and, if you'll so indulge me, stories whispered by stone and soil alike. It is said that every grave bears two epitaphs—the one etched in bronze and the one left unwritten, floating between memory and regret. Here, among these hallowed grounds, you will find both.

I suppose you are here for me to guide you through this sanctified domain. Very well. The air may be heavy with incense and the quiet hum of prayers, but listen closer, and you'll hear the faint murmur of secrets—the stories that linger long after the last "amen."

Saint Ambrose has a way of holding onto its own, you see. Be it the devout or the damned, the innocent or the guilty, they all find their place here eventually. And yet, for some, the grave cannot contain the weight of what they carried in life. Their tales bleed into these walls, this earth, this air—asking to be heard, or perhaps, warning others not to tread the same path.

Do not be afraid, though uneasiness is natural when you realize the dead often have more to say than the living. "Eternal rest," they say. Let me show you the epitaphs that only the restless can leave behind. For in Saint Ambrose, every shadow tells a tale, and every tale has a place.

PROUD

*E*mployment at Saint Ambrose can be awful, filthy work. Oh, I do not mean this in regard to our dealings with the deceased, mind you. While the dead do not pick up after themselves, they are not the ones responsible for the atrocious messes one has to clean up in the normal course of a day. They are innocent bystanders… or by-liers, I suppose one could say, at least for the most part.

Matthew sought me out not long ago, wanting to assist in some of the routine maintenance and cleaning, in particular that of the mausoleum. A peculiar request from such a sweet lad, really. A bit light in the head, but he took to his work with the utmost vigor. Worked well into the evenings, he did. Said it was all to help his house-bound father, the dear boy. A shame I could not pay him but a pittance.

Alas, Matthew confided in me, in his own way of speaking, that money was of little matter to him. At the end of the night, what mattered most to Matthew—Matty, as he opted to be called—was that his hard work would do most to make his father proud.

Matty pried the nickel from the floor with a badly trimmed thumbnail. The coin didn't come off very easily, caked with weeks of grime and whatever else sticks to the bottom of shoes nice enough for polish. He was holding a whole minute in his hand, if he made three dollars an hour. *PopPop would be so proud of me*, Matty thought, regarding more the nickel than his maths.

He rolled the coin over in his even filthier hands to admire Jefferson's profile, though Matty didn't know who that was. Matty knew the man on a nickel looked like PopPop, and that made him smile. He swirled his blackened thumb across PopPop's face in hopes to clean him off, but it had little effect.

"Into the bucket, PopPop," Matty said to the nickel, and he tossed it overhand into the wheeled pail of steaming, grey mop water. The *ploop-clank* made Matty laugh. His guffaw echoed down the bouquet-lined, marble hallway, multiplying like a crowd of himself.

Two points! PopPop would be so proud of me.

Matty ran the wet string mop across the floor, passing over the nickel-shaped void left behind. *The floor has a spot just like the ones PopPop gave me*, thought Matty. *But floors don't itch when it gets hot outside.*

"Ashtray," Matty said, eyeing the spot on his left arm. "PopPop says time to play ashtray, Mister Floor." He laughed again, softly to himself.

PopPop loved games. He loved basketball so much that Matty saw him pay lots of money to his friend, Bookie, to watch every week. He loved football and boxing. And he loved ashtray.

Placing the mop back into water that was now looking much more dirty than clean, Matty rolled the bucket to the ladies' lavatory. He pressed his back to the door to enter, hesitating with his usual wave of shame.

"Knock, knock," Matty said to the vacant room. "Matty's here. Matty won't peek!"

"You respect your sister, Matty," PopPop used to say. "Respect the ladies, for Chrissakes, and I won't have to take my cane to the back of your big, retarded head all the time when you're all gawkin' like that."

PopPop would be so proud right now.

Matty took a tray of cleaners to the sinks and turned them both on hot. The steam created its usual veil on the mirrors, obscuring his reflection—just what Matty wanted. He never liked the man in the mirrors. A head too large for his body, his face appearing as though melted and rehardened. The steam made the room stuffy, and Matty reached up to scratch the newly developing itch on his cheek.

"You're a goddamn animal, Matty," said PopPop. "A filthy pig. It's time I really clean your disgusting, piggy face." PopPop always loved calling Matty funny names like that. Matty turned the sinks off and used the cleaners and cloths to scrub their ins and outs. He took out what he called "shiny spray" and gave the handles a hefty polish. Matty's reflection was there, but tiny, bendy Matty only served to make him laugh.

"Good job, little Matty," Matty said to his tiny self, admiring how well the special spray did the job. *PopPop would be so proud.*

Matty entered the first toilet stall with the bottles and brush. He stared blankly at the seat, already lifted up. "Only custodial peoples lift ladies seats," he said, then smothered a giggle with his elbow pit. "Or boys."

He got down on his knees, just like he used to see his sister Molly do in the last days he saw her, living with PopPop. Only she'd be leaning over and making awful sounds inside it.

"Your sister's sick," PopPop told Matty on those days. "She's dyin', and she's the only one smart enough in this goddamn house to earn their keep."

"I'll get a job, PopPop," Matty said. "I'll make you proud."

"You!? A job? You're a retard. I'd be proud if you could wipe your own ass."

That night Matty learned to use the toilet and the paper all by himself, when Molly was done using it. Molly was done using the toilet for good. PopPop didn't say so, but Matty was sure he was proud of him now.

Matty hummed a nondescript tune as he worked. He would whistle, but he never learned how, and PopPop said you needed all your teeth to whistle. He scoured both bowls with his brush but didn't flush. He liked to keep the water blue and sudsy; he wanted ladies coming in the next day to know that Matty had done a good job.

Matty didn't like the men's room. He didn't like the toilets where some boys stood only to pee. He didn't like the letters scribbled on the grey-painted stall walls, with a marker Matty could barely rub off. He especially didn't like the smell.

Matty took a rag and rubbing alcohol to the first stall and worked at removing the fresh insults written there in black.

"You good-for-nothing mongoloid!" PopPop used to say when he wasn't happy with Matty. "Did you pour my goddamn vodka in the sink?"

"Yes, PopPop," said Matty. "Molly used to—"

"Don't you ever speak your sister's name in this house again, boy!" PopPop's cane contacted with Matty's jaw, dislodging a tooth and sending the whistle impairment skittering across the kitchen floor.

"The bottle wasn't empty, you idiot!" PopPop yelled. "Fuuh-king retard. I wish your sister was here to see how much dumber you are now. Your ugly, stupid ass still can't even spell!"

"Sh—Shit," Marty sounded out as the final profane word faded beneath his cloth. He sounded out the word but gave no meaning to it, yet he smiled just the same.

PopPop, you would be so proud.

Matty's job was done. "Another day, another dollar. Shaquille O'Neal, one foot taller." PopPop used to say that all the time. It made Matty laugh just to say it to himself, and the hundreds of name-plated doors echoed in return.

Matty snatched the nickel from the emptied mop bucket. "There you are, PopPop," Matty said to the now-glistening face, then pocketed it. He retrieved a large, full trash bag and slung it over a shoulder, then closeted the cleaning things and exited out the building's back entrance. The rotting smell of dumpster foulness outside was immediate, having baked in a summer sun for hours. To Matty, it smelled like dying.

Last week, Matty had finally entered his father's bedroom, having not seen the man emerge for two days.

"PopPop, you—you don't smell good," Matty said. Beams of light filtered through week-old cigar smoke, falling across the oc-cupied bed in a zebra-like pattern, barely lighting the man-shaped heap of bedsheets. Breathable air was overcome by the stench of rotting fecal matter, body odor, and stale booze.

"Matty," PopPop's voice barely creaked, from the fe-tal-positioned lump on the bed. "You—you good-for-nothing mong—mongoloid."

"PopPop, are you gonna be okay?" Matty asked.

PopPop waited a while to answer. If he moved at all, Matty could not tell. "No, I'm not okay. I'm never gonna be okay, Matty. You're here, and your—your sister's not. I'm barely here. I've got nothing. Nothing left."

The sheets pulled in tighter and jerked in short spasms as Pop-Pop choked back tears and whatever else his body wanted to expel.

"What can I do, PopPop?" asked Matty.

"Nothing!" PopPop barked in a phlegmy voice. "I want my little girl back, not you. I want Molly."

A bout of hollow coughs belted forth then from the bed, followed by the distinct sound and smell of acidic vomit. PopPop's form did little in the way of movement, then all went silent.

Matty's walk home was short but tiring, and he was thankful for the quiet, lonely, late-night streets. He unlocked and opened the front door with an exhausted hand, then slumped with his belongings on the couch. Arching back, he pulled the nickel from his pocket.

"PopPop," Matty said out loud in the empty room. "You'll be so proud of me, PopPop."

Matty returned to his feet and lifted the large bag from near where he sat. He carried it and himself to the nearest bedroom, then flung the heavy load onto the still-occupied bed. Its contents spilled out in a heap of foul-smelling clothes and decay.

"I did what you wanted, PopPop. I went to work at the fancy, marbly place we put Molly in. I took her out, and I brought her back for you."

PopPop did not move, nor had his position changed for days. What had changed was the smell: the fetor of decaying flesh, now twofold.

"I did a good job cleaning up after myself—and everything else—like a real janitor would do. Like you, PopPop! Matty's no piggy!"

Matty fell into bed and lay between the only family he'd ever known.

"You're proud of Matty now, right, PopPop?"

CHYANDOUR

Mrs. Sophie Finnegan has a special sort of residency here in the mausoleum. You see, while a fine-polished, bronze plate adorns her tomb of eternal rest, the space beyond its door will remain forever empty. The same cannot be said for her dear husband, Charles, however. While he, too, maintains the same fine accommodations alongside the missus, his presence is here, in perpetuity, perhaps forever unaccompanied.

The mausoleum has become quite populated, and while I have tried to reason with the Finnegan family in freeing up the unoccupied vault, they would hear of no such thing. Perhaps it is comforting to them to know she still has a place. Until then, I imagine she will still and forevermore take residence nearby their former summer lake house, a place they once took to calling Chyandour.

Morning has not been kind to me lately. I'm not sure I can say we've ever quite seen eye to eye, morning and me. She's just being more of a bitch than usual these days. She's a vicious reminder that my desperate attempt at sleep has ended; daylight is here and, with it, the rest of the waking world. Expecting things from me. Expecting my full attention. Because, after all, I've had a restful sleep, haven't I? That's what they assume. That's what they have to assume. Otherwise, I've got nothing. I'm out on my ass.

But the morning isn't all bad. For her, night makes way. For me, night has been the cruelest bastard of all. Ginger, I know, feels the same way. Though, unlike me, she gets to sleep all day.

Ginger is my three-year-old Shepherd. Since late last November, she and I have more or less been on the same sleepless, nighttime schedule. There are times when knowing she's laying alert at the foot of my bed gets me a few moments of eye resting, but not often. My wife, meanwhile, sleeps through the night like a stone. As far as she's concerned, I'm dealing with an extended bout of insomnia, most likely due to stress of the job. If that were only true. But I won't tell her the real reason. I can't. Our son can't afford to have us both losing our minds. Not again.

She can't know what happened last time at Chyandour.

Katy fell in love with the place. The moment she crossed the threshold, that was it. Five years ago. It was a summer so hot and dry the lake dropped nearly two feet, and swimming in it felt like a bath. The house belonged to my grandfather, who'd passed away that spring and left it for my mother and her sister—my aunt Rita—to grapple over. It wasn't much of a fight, really. Aunt Rita wanted nothing to do with it. She said Chyandour was a closet of bad memories she was keen on keeping shut. My parents, meanwhile, had since moved to Florida, and while they didn't outright gift the house to me when they left, I'd been given license to make use of it any time I liked. Thirty acres. The entire western coastline.

But Chyandour was never my thing. Chyandour: a name my grandmother gave the house, decades ago, when he first had it built. That's the sort of thing people sometimes do with houses along bodies of water. Like boats and ships, they're given names. You could suppose it gives a house some quaint character, making it more of an exclusive destination than simply calling it "The Lake House" or "The Charles Finnegan House" after my grandfather. But a name. A name gives it a soul. For better or worse.

From the outside, the house isn't very remarkable. Being in the middle of nowhere, it really doesn't have to be. Northern weather resiliency is all that's key. Its façade is shingled in unpainted cedar, its roof aluminum panels with the stains and dents from years of wear. A large, screened turret sits adjacent to the kitchen, overlooking the wooden footpath, the large dock and beach far below. And beyond, the Pakniwat, a hundred-acre lake surrounded mostly by uninhabited conservation woodlands, and then the large, lonely plot Chyandour sits upon.

The surrounding area is what contributes to the beauty of the location, not the accommodations. For such a large piece of property, the house is rather small. About nine hundred square feet, which is certainly respectable for a part-time home. But when you're up to inviting friends and family to spend the weekend, it can get rather—let's just say—cozy. And that's just how Grammy wanted it: cozy. So that's how my grandfather built it. For a rather introverted couple like Katy and me, and not up for inviting people along on our trips, it was just about right. Kids on one floor, adults on the other. Cozy when we wanted to be, blissfully distant when not.

Still, woodland living was never for me. I'm not a city boy by any means, but to be so removed from the rest of the world feels disconcerting, to say the least. Sometimes, when the air becomes still and the birds haven't yet awoken, it's not just quiet: it's silent. There is nothing. And while I'm fine being alone, I am not fond of being lonely. And that's just what being at Chyandour alone made me feel: lonely.

Though the house isn't mine, per se, I hold all the responsibility for its upkeep. It's only fair; we're the only people making use of it. Winterizing the place was the last item to be checked off every year, and I'd been doing it for four. It's not something

I ever look forward to doing. I loathe the cold. Though this past year, after what had happened last summer, I was up for avoiding it altogether. I was up for never going back to Chyandour again.

Ginger and I pulled into the dirt driveway very early on a Friday. I had to burn a day of vacation in order to beat the northbound traffic, hoping to avoid the carloads of leaf-peepers that'd be clogging the highways and making the already miserable trip worse. I had the office reschedule all my patients for the following week. I hated the fact that I was blowing a vacation day on something like this more than how swamped I'd be when I got back.

The ground was thoroughly littered in leaves. Every tree apart from firs and pines were bare to the bark. This far north, autumn had already passed through. The roof of the house was also a blanket of colorful foliage. Cleaning it off to prevent ice dams and roof collapse was one the chores on my to-do list for the weekend. I had plenty to keep myself busy for a couple of days.

When I opened the front door, Ginger got right to work sniffing about the place as usual. The house had its own smell to it, one I can only describe as "stale cabin." I guess every new house you enter, or one you hadn't seen the inside of for months, has its own smell that you tend to get used to and not notice over time. Like boiled cabbage that's seeped into the walls and carpets for over a century, or flowery air fresheners that waft throughout every room and cling like oil to every surface. Chyandour was stale cabin.

It was a mild day for November, and I was glad for the opportunity to throw some windows open and air the place out. I opened the door to the turret porch and stepped outside. Warm air filtered through the floor-to-roof screened walls, and through my nose I welcomed it deeply and filled my lungs. Early morning sun glittered upon the lake like diamonds dancing upon the water. Far below, the wooden dock extended outward, twenty feet from shore, its planks somehow kept bare and free of the fallen leaves.

I could see him lying there. Not presently. This wasn't summer, and it wasn't five months ago. In my mind I could still see Jake as I'd seen him last. Arms crossed behind his head as a makeshift pillow, legs linked at the ankles with one foot dancing to music only he could hear. The cords of headphones snaked from his ears to the small music player laying nearby. His usually pale skin already bronzing from the long stretch of cloudless days under a hot, July sun. We'd told him countless times to wear sunscreen, but on vacation you tend to let up on the rules.

He was thirteen, only a fragment of worries of the world in his head.

Ginger sidled up beside me, interested at the moment in what was taking my attention. She stared down below and whimpered, as though she knew what I was feeling, or recalling her own memories of Jake. But this wasn't some movie where things like that tend to happen, and I know dogs better than that. I swiped my jacket sleeve across my eyes, unpacked her bag of kibble, and filled her bowl. I took the other bowl to the sink to fill with water. When I returned, the food bowl was still untouched, and Ginger was still where I'd left her in the porch. But she was whimpering.

I spent the morning raking leaves, pine needles, and fallen pinecones. A blanket nearly a foot thick clung to the roof despite it being angled. The deck was much worse, and rain from the previous week made everything wet and heavy. And dirty. Ginger joined me outside, no doubt desperate for a walk but enjoying biding her time gnawing on the largest stick she could find. The work sounds miserable, and for the most part it is, but you don't get many fall days like that. Looking down at the beautiful palette of colors scattered about the ground, some carried away by the growing winds of an incoming front, it gets you remembering why some say this is the best part of the world to live in. If it wasn't so God-damned isolated, I'd be saying that myself. So I enjoy of it what I can, when I can.

With the leaves clear, the last bit of outside work was putting the canoe into storage. Just as we did all summer, it'd been left upside-down near the small beach. If I was being lazy, I could have left it there and it would probably be in the same place come spring. Probably. There was always the real risk of the lake rising higher than anticipated due to heavy snowfall, which would take said canoe on a ride of its own. That happened to our last canoe, and we never saw it again. Like many things, the lake took it into the depths of herself.

Ginger and I took the walk down to the dock together. I brought a few of the sticks she was chewing with me, and she hopped in anticipation of me throwing one of them for her to fetch. She loved the water, and the swimming would do good in tiring her out. I cranked my arm back to throw, and Ginger took off in the direction I was aiming. I released, and the stick sailed end-over-end toward the water, just far enough out for Ginger to make a safe swim to it, but not too close to be easy. She reached the end of the dock and leapt in without hesitation. A cold chill ran through my body in thinking of how frigid that water must be. There's no testing of the waters for a dog. It's dive right in, water's fine.

I got to the end of the dock just as I saw Ginger's head gliding above the water, about five feet from the stick. As though distracted by something, she turned around and started to head back to shore. I thought maybe she couldn't see it.

"Girly-girl, get the stick! Go get it!"

Her ears perked up, and she turned back around. This time she got closer to the stick, but again she turned back around and whimpered. It wasn't as though it was too far for her to reach.

"Go on! Get it, Ginger!"

I threw another stick. This one splashed down within her path, closer to shore. She wasn't interested. She passed the stick and made her way to the beach.

"Ginger! What's up?"

She paid me no mind and turned to face the lake. She sat down in the wet leaves and sand, staring out to where ripples still lapped away from her wake and from the sticks I'd thrown. She hadn't even taken a moment to shake off the water that matted down her fur. She cried again. Maybe the cold water had gotten to her after all. Or could it be that she remembered? Could a dog replay the day in her own head like I'd been cursed to do for the past five months?

Damn you, girl. In my mind's eye, I saw it too. Still, none of it makes sense. Jake is a skilled swimmer for his age. We trust him to know what he's doing. He must have had enough of the sun and jumped in. One desperate yell for help, and then he's gone. Ginger leapt in. I followed. We treaded water for so long we almost went under for good.

He didn't come up. Not minutes later. Not hours. Not days. Not ever. Other than the wet puddle he'd left upon the dock where he'd been laying, we never saw sign of our oldest boy again. Not unless it's like now, in memories sometimes best forgotten.

"Where did you go, Jake? God damn it, where did you go?"

More whimpering. This time it's me.

The opposite shore was still bright and warm as it undertook the last of the daylight. True to a northern autumn, the cold fell fast upon the shadowed western bank. I brought an armload of firewood inside the house and in twenty minutes had the stove roaring. Ginger had since dried off. After finally eating, she coiled herself into a tight ball by the fire and promptly passed out. Being back at this place must have taken a toll on the poor girl. I felt like passing out myself. But it was still early, and I had more things to do before turning in. I was intent on getting out of there the next day and not spending another night. If I had my way, I'd be happy not going back ever again.

I finished most of the interior winterizing by about ten o'clock. All that was left was draining the pipes to prevent them from splitting in the eventual sub-zero temps. But I still had another morning to come, and I preferred a flushing toilet. Though isolated, the house had its own water supply, a cistern situated up on the hillside, kept full with rain water, melting snow, and the occasional gas-powered siphoning from the lake. What we didn't have was electricity, except when we threw the generator on in desperate times. Apart from cell phones with weak signals, we were kept completely off the grid. Katy considered us blissfully incommunicado. To me, we were disconcertingly secluded.

I wish I could say I crashed for the night, that I slept like a log—or a dog, as the case may be. It just wasn't going to happen. Not without help. I pulled the bottle of Laphroaig cask-strength out of my stash in the closet, emptied it neat into a glass. Three fingers. Closer to four. I knocked it all back in one go. It was a shame to treat it that way, but I was ready to be knocked on my ass right quick. There seemed to be no other way.

Splash.

"DAD!"

My head flew up from the table and my arm caught the empty whiskey bottle, sending it flying onto the floor.

"Jake?! Jacob?!"

The unbroken bottle continued to roll about on the hardwood while my own voice still echoed in my throbbing head. My throat was on fire. How long had I been yelling?

Damn it. God damn it.

I wanted to call Katy. I needed to. I wiped the string of spittle that clung to the table to my mouth and pulled out my cell. The time read about two-thirty. No signal. It wouldn't matter, though. She slept like the dead and would wake up for nothing. I couldn't let it get to me again, though. I'd have to forget what had happened. I had to sleep.

I managed to make my way to the sink, splashed water on my face, and took long gulps of it with cupped hands. The house, the water—all of it is freezing cold. I packed the fireplace tight with new logs. Soon it's again dangerous and hot, and the uncomfortable chill began to dissolve.

The bed was already occupied by the dog. I let it slide, as I always do. She knew this and didn't budge. Katy's not there, or sometimes it'd be Jake or Wil when one of them couldn't fall asleep. I was happy to let her stay.

I killed the only lantern I'd lit and slid between the glacial bedsheets. Bronze shadows danced upon the living room walls by the glow through the soot-stained window of the stove. It didn't take long to feel the onset of sleep again. I rested and thought of nothing other than welcoming it, as Ginger already had.

I was awakened not long after by what I believed was a light. I could sense brightness as my lids reddened over my shut eyes, though once I cracked them open, there was nothing. I faced the sliding doors to the outside, the moonless sky beyond and the still lake far below. No sound other than the muffled crackling of burning wood from the stove in the next room. I brushed it off as nothing. I was overtired.

Minutes later, as I was just drifting off again, Ginger's head shot up, ears perked, on alert. She'd heard something. That got my attention, and my eyes became saucers. And I'm listening. But there is nothing. Nothing for a long while. Ginger shuffled off the bed and walked into the living room to investigate. I figured that's what dogs are for and let her be. The tip-tap of her paws upon the floor grew distant, toward the front door by the kitchen. *Maybe she's just cold*, I think, *and she's back by the fire*. More likely she has to pee.

I waited for her usual scratch at the door, but it never came. Instead, a low snarl. It's my girly-girl, not some wild beast of the night or a thing unexplained. What wasn't explained is what had upset her, and like a coward I kept the bed covers pulled tight to my chin and lay silently in wait. Her growling continued for minutes more, never escalating to a bark. Just a raccoon or opossum, rummaging in the trash I'd left outside to take home? That time of year, it could've been a deer, perhaps, or even a bear. In normal circumstances, I am not such a pussy. In normal circumstances, I'm not alone—not at Chyandour. I'm not normally so exhausted by an afternoon of beating back vivid memories of my missing child, of so many fallen tears my shirt could be wrung out of them.

Ginger quieted. I could only assume that whatever she'd heard was gone, and I was for the moment relieved. The bed lurched as she leapt back into it. This time she crawled closer beside me, prone against my back. She let out a drawn-out sigh, and that alone was the comfort I needed to feel at peace. She snuggled closer, and I sighed of contentment myself.

The growling started again. Not from the bed. Just outside the bedroom door.

Tip-tap. Tip-tap.

It's my girly-girl. It's Ginger. And I thought, *How did I not notice her getting off the bed again?* Except she didn't.

The body next to me moved. I was suddenly frightened to the point I could vomit, and I felt the bed begin to dampen beneath me. I considered my options. Pretend I'm asleep and let my dog scare away whatever is in the bed with me? Toss the blankets aside and make break for the sliding door? I was not going anywhere. Fear paralyzed me.

"Come..." it said, a voice that was of command, not suggestion. The air was suddenly fetid.

I hate this place! I hate it! I hate it! Go away!

The thing beside me made a sound like a hiss, as though displeased with my thoughts. A weight was lifted from the bed as whatever it was slid away and onto the floor. But there were no footfalls, only Ginger's continued growls. A long shadow grew upon the wall. It was tall, not like one the dog would cast or any other sort of smaller animal. The form seemed human.

Please just go away. Leave me alone. I wanted to say all of this, but I only dared to purse my eyelids shut.

Tip. Tap.

Ginger was just inside the room. She started barking, with a voice that said, "Get the fuck out of here now or I'll kill you," that this was no warning but a very sincere order. I heard the sliding glass door open, then shut. Ginger barreled into the room, still barking with increasing ferocity. Standing on her hind legs, she pawed at the glass door to be let out, wanting to make sure whoever or whatever had intruded on us was gone for good. It was then that I had the nerve to get out of bed, to chance at seeing the trespasser flee off the side of the balcony and into the night. It was much too dark to see a thing. Then I heard it.

Splash.

In an instant and for a quick moment, bright light filled the room from every window. It seemed to come from all directions, with an intensity such that I had to shield my eyes from being blinded. Even Ginger was stunned, and she whined with shock. Without a sound it was gone, before either of us had time to adjust.

I immediately set about the house locking the doors and windows, something I hadn't felt the need to do before, as removed from civilization as Chyandour was. I discovered the front door ajar. My hands were shaking so badly they were barely able to operate the deadbolts. My legs were rubber, clothing soaked. I steadied myself against my knees, caught my breath, and stared longingly at the empty bottle on the floor. I wished it was full.

I fell backward onto my ass, pulled my legs up to my chest. Ginger sat beside me, as I wept until the sun came up.

Roughly an hour later, I was able to pose as someone pulling themselves together. The bed, I saw, was still a mess, just as I'd left it. Still wet. The comforter, the sheets, the mattress—even the box spring—were drenched through to the floor. That wasn't from me. Along the opposite side of the bed I slept on: the unmistakable, wet silhouette of a person. I was baffled as to what to make of it. Ginger sniffed at it and whimpered. She walked over to the glass doors and stared out at the lake for a moment, then looked back at me expectantly.

"What's up, girly-girl? Need to go out?"

She cried again. I went to the back door, unlatched the lock. Ginger pushed her way past me, through the door and outside, before I had it open an inch. I watched her scramble down the footpath, not to the nearby woods where she usually did her business. Instead, she made her way to the end of the dock and sat, facing the open water that was as still as a mirror.

I can't get over how she misses him. She was Jake's dog, after all. And Jake was her person. But she wasn't by the water because she missed her boy. Not this time.

Her ears were pinned back, the hair on her back raised. I could hear her growling again.

I packed up what I needed and hit the road. Physically and emotionally, I was spent. In my condition, driving was not the best of ideas, but there was no way I would stay longer than I had to. Ginger crashed in the back seat. I'm sure she was just as glad to be gone.

Relief washed over me when the tires finally hit the pavement of Main Street. My cell began to ring. A still image of Katy's smiling face graced my phone's screen.

"Hey," I said.

"Hey. You already on your way home?"

"Yeah. I've got one more thing to do first. Should be home in a few hours."

"Okay. Wil and I are anxious to see you. You... feeling okay? You sound exhausted."

"I am exhausted. But I'll be fine. Can't wait to see you guys."

"Please drive safe, okay? Pull over if you have to."

"Okay. I might do that. See you soon."

I hung up and glanced at the empty passenger seat beside me.

I wish we didn't have to go home. I wish we could stay there forever.

"I know you do, buddy."

Dad?

"Yeah, Jake?"

Why do you hate the lake house so much?

I thought back to what Aunt Rita had told me long ago. The truth of why she hoped to never again set eyes upon that place. What my mother had so long denied happening and refused to believe. That, should we return, to be sure to never be alone while along the shore of Lake Pakniwat. To never be taken in by that greedy, evil place.

"Because Chyandour takes those that love it too much, Jake. Never lets go of them. Like it took you. Like it took grammy. And I won't let it take your brother. Or Mom."

The first gas station was another mile ahead. Filling the three empty canisters in the trunk should be enough to do the job.

THE REAPING OF BOBBY WARD

Everyone deserves to be loved, respected... until they don't. There are those who strangely seek out recognition at any expense, even at the cost of the respect they so desperately desire. To what means, I wonder? All to wind up here, behind a sealed door of marble, remarked only with what epitaph fits upon a sixteen-inch sheet of polished bronze.

Will you be forever remembered for your deeds, either good or bad? Is that perhaps some solace to those who go to great lengths to achieve the notoriety they feel they so deserve? I suppose it all depends on what story is being told of one's past, whether it be one of inspiration to others or as a word of warning. One particular case of the latter comes to mind, the subject of which lies within these walls. Dear residents of Eastboro and nearby towns would deny the occurrence, of course. Deny it or not, I'm quite sure they would very much like to forget the reaping of Bobby Ward.

I've already lived a life full of stories to tell. It's true that I tend to get repetitive from time to time, though I don't think that means I'm losing my marbles so soon, or at least I certainly hope not. Subconscious avoidance is more like it. Cut out disturbing memory, copy-paste something else over it. There are times when I wish some of my memories were less interesting. My wife will tell you that they're all of the mundane variety; she just hasn't heard them all yet.

Like the one about the Grim Reaper.

Most everyone's heard of at least of some kind of embodiment of Death. The Grim Reaper's a top choice for most folks. The guy who carries a big scythe, who we all imagine stands dark and tall, hooded and cloaked, probably with a fleshless skull where a head should be. Maybe he's got a bony finger peeking out from his sleeve, beckoning you with it or chastising you or whatever he does when he's pointing at you.

The Grim Reaper's a scary guy, all right, but he's not exactly the type of scary guy you might imagine running after you with his blade swinging over his head all propeller-like, screaming like some maniac in the night. No, I think most folks think the Reaper's presence alone is enough to scare the ever-living—or ever-dying, as the case may be—shit out of you. Most of the time, in his most frightening form, he just stands there, motionless.

Most of the time.

Summer vacation from high school in the mid-'80s in a small New England town tended to be as boring as watching warts grow on a toad. Outside of watching television, home-based electronic entertainment was a luxury most of us couldn't yet afford, and without access to a set of wheels other than a bicycle, we were more or less forced to be creative for entertainment.

Dave McGrath was a year older than me and, as far as anyone knew, was relatively friendless. I didn't go out of my way to befriend the guy to the point of best-friendiness, though I certainly didn't try to avoid him. Dave had just gotten his driver's license that summer. That made Dave, to me, a convenient acquaintance. Unfortunately, a driver's license doesn't automatically come with transportation, so my celebration of that fact was short-lived.

I'd known Dave for a few years while thoroughly warming the bench together for the Peasley High varsity basketball team. We both had something peculiar in common: we were both tall, and we both royally sucked at basketball. The only reason we made the cut at tryouts was because there were no cuts; there simply weren't enough kids trying out. Our most useful contribution was helping intimidate other schools by increasing the team's visible height average.

Sitting on the bench for a high school varsity sports team felt a lot like the summer of Dave's driver's license. Facing us was possibility of a marked increase in our popularity, but instead we were met with the halting palm of denial.

Popularity does not always beget desirability. As if to prove to us that point, Dave's asshole of a neighbor pulled up in his own '81 Chevy Camaro one summer night, as Dave and I shot hoops in the street. I swear on my sweet mother's grave, that bastard could sniff out disappointment and despair from miles away and make sure he'd be present in time to enjoy the show, symbolic popcorn in hand.

Said asshole, Bobby Ward, never left high school life and mentality behind, despite being a first-year at Harlan Community College. He hated the summer, partly because it meant he couldn't wear his corduroy varsity letter jacket around the Harlan campus without trailing a stream of sweat in his path. He was still convinced of its ability to show he was a hotter shit than you, even though

Harlan was half-populated with fellow graduates from Peasley. "Peasley two-point-oh," they called it. There was little point in trying to bullshit those who were aware of our school's varsity standards, but he knocked himself out.

Mostly, though, Bobby hated summer because he was a big guy. He wasn't as tall as Dave, but he pushed close to three bills, a higher percentage of that not being muscle and bone. That didn't mean he looked any less intimidating, something he took advantage of on a regular basis. Bobby was fond of insults, pranks, and overall general discomfort at any level, especially if he was the one administering it. Unfortunately for Dave, living in close proximity to such a lout meant he was one of Bobby's primary sources of entertainment.

As God is my witness, the bastard was actually eating fucking popcorn when he pulled up.

The Camaro's tinted passenger-side window rolled down halfway. I took a half-assed shot from the foul line as Bobby leaned across from the driver's seat. His fat face flashed a shit-eating grin, his full mouth still munching as he called out to us.

"Hey! You guys want to see something wicked fucked up?"

There were three others in the car with Bobby. His much-younger brother, John, sat back in the passenger seat, shielding his face from the spittle issuing from his left. In the back were two others I didn't recognize, but they all seemed in about the same age range as the rest of us.

Dave was usually extremely apprehensive to get anywhere close to Bobby Ward, let alone when he was behind the controls of machinery. Getting within arm's reach of a quintessential bully like Bobby was seen as an invitation for an instant debagging, or worse. Maybe then it was a sudden onset of delirium brought on by the dry summer heat that caused Dave to call back in reply.

"I guess so."

My jaw dropped, along with my missed shot. "Let's go. Get in."

The passenger door flew open. The two kids in back slid aside to make room.

"Don't mind those idiots," Bobby said, motioning to the back seat. "Those're my cousins, Paul and Greg. We just got back from seeing *Fright Night*, and these pussies thought it was scary!" He said "scary" as "scaya-wee," in that "aw, poor baby" tone that's specially reserved for parents of newborns and demeaning shitheels.

"Nuh-uh!" protested one of the cousins.

The shaming tone of Bobby's voice seemed to snap Dave back into his usual, hesitant self and take a slight step back. "Why? Where are you going now?" he asked.

Bobby took a break from shoveling seed into his mouth. "You guys ever hear of the Grim Reaper?"

"What, the band?" I asked.

"The band? You retard! No! I mean the guy, the Grim Reaper. The one with the big axe!"

"It's a scythe," Dave corrected.

"Pssh! What-the-fuck ever! Scythe, big-ass axe. Yeah, him."

"Okay," said Dave. "What about him?"

"Let's go. Get in. You'll see."

Approximately thirty seconds later, it started to sink in that we'd just crawled into the back seat of this tubby lug's car and let him drive away with us. Apparently to see Death himself, no less.

The granite quarry was only about three miles from Dave and Bobby's neighborhood, though the rough ride there felt like twenty. I'd heard of lots of kids sneaking off there to swim, drink, and smoke, oftentimes being chased away by town cops. Whether they were rumors or not, stories flew of people from other towns jumping off the fifty-foot ledges into the frigid, spring-fed water below, drowning or never resurfacing. Some said they were diving down too deep, drunk or high, getting stuck in one of the many sunken trucks or various other large pieces of junk. Worse stories told of witnessing seagulls feasting on body parts that had washed up onto stone ridges along the quarry walls. True or not, those tales were enough to keep my ass planted at a beach when I needed cooling off.

Bobby lit a cigarette from a Zippo as he slowed the Camaro to a crawl, taking the turn onto the quarry road. From a cracked and pot-holed road, the car dropped several inches onto the narrow gravel path.

"Okay, I have to slow down," Bobby said. "He's up along this road somewhere, and we might miss him."

"Who is?" asked Greg, to my left.

"The Grim Reaper, moron!" said Bobby.

"Bullshit!" said Paul.

"I shit you not! There is this guy, okay? And he walks on this road at night, looks just like him. He's tall as shit, all dressed in a brown cloak. Carries a big fucking wheat-chopper."

"Get the fuck out of here," I said in disbelief.

"Hey, you'll see. He's up here somewhere. Keep an eye out. I'll check the left side. Johnny, you check the right."

Bobby continued to drive at walking speed while grunting the guitar riff from "Smoke on the Water." The rest of us kept our mouths shut and our eyes wide.

Several minutes into the crawl down the path I asked, "Who told you about this guy?"

"Saw him myself," Bobby replied in almost a whisper. "I took a chick up here last week, y'know, to fuck and stuff."

Paul burst out laughing at that. "Shyeah, right!"

"Shut up, jerk-off!" Bobby blasted, reaching back in an attempt to swat at his cousin's head. "Anyway, we come up around a corner, and there's this huge guy. I mean huge! I didn't know what he was gonna do—maybe cut my fuckin' dick off—so I got the fuck out of there faster than Paul spooges beating off."

"I don't—Fuck you, Bobby," Paul said.

"Sshh, shh, shh! Shut up, guys!" Bobby's brother interrupted. "Bobby, is this the place?"

"Oh. Yeah, yeah. We're almost to the spot. He was… right around…"

When reacting to terror, you can be undaunted and fearless, perhaps even brave; you can be cowering and terrified, or just extremely guarded; or you can be "jump-scared." Regardless of whether or not you are naturally fearless or terrified, if something catches you by surprise, you're going to be jump-scared. Case in point: the driver of a carload of wary teenagers blasting into abrupt, chaotic cacophony from near-dead silence.

Bobby yelled with such force that his voice cracked. *"HOLY SHIT THERE HE IS! HE'S RIGHT THERE!"*

"THERE HE IS! GET OUT OF HERE!" John joined in. "GO, BOBBY! GET OUT! DRIVE!"

In the back seat, we didn't know what the hell was going on, but we were all jump-scared shitless, regardless. This time I mean the term "shitless" literally, as it was clear that someone in the car had loosened their bowels. All of this happened before any of the rest of us had made visual contact with whatever the Ward boys were carrying on about.

Then I saw him. About fifty yards away, abutting the woods on the right side of the road, was the unmistakable shape of a towering, hooded figure. From that distance, he looked to be eight feet tall, carrying a very tall staff of some kind. The shape of the cloak was tattered and jagged, its hood covering and darkening anything behind.

The car's headlights filtered through the branches close to the road as they blew in the increasing winds. Shadows swept across the tree line, and the cloaked shape appeared to turn its head in our direction. The persistent, loud yelling and overpowering stench of fresh shit in the air made it difficult to think straight. The rush of adrenaline caused my throat to constrict and my eyes to water and burn.

The Wards continued to scream and point out the windshield. The rest of us pushed back into our seats. Bobby accelerated the car forward.

"What the hell are you doing?!" yelled Greg, or maybe Paul. "Turn around! TURN AROUND!"

The Camaro sped through the dirt, closer to what sure as hell looked like the Grim Reaper, big-ass axe and all. He was huge, taller than he appeared from where we first saw him. The wind continued to whip through the trees.

The massive scythe shifted in its grasp. Others in the back seat cowered away from the passenger side, as though shifting themselves over by a foot would help save them from something intent on crashing through an already speeding car with its fleshless hands.

I plastered my face against the window in order to see his full height. With the headlights no longer illuminating him, I could only make out its distinct outline, that of a cloak and scythe. As we passed within a few yards of the thing, Bobby pulled the steering wheel counter-clockwise and fishtailed the car to face in the other direction, slamming everyone against the passenger side of the car.

The Ward brothers ceased their yelling almost as quickly as they'd started, as we sped away from the quarry. Then, joining the sound of the Camaro's engine, came the sound of their snickering. Bobby punctuated the moment with his own coughed-out guffaw.

"You... you," Bobby managed to sputter in between gasps for breath and gagging on cigarette smoke. "You guys... shit yourselves! I mean, you literally, honest-to-God shit your pants, you were so scared!"

For a moment, no one else spoke. I think the rest us were letting sink in what had just happened, even though we still were not sure what that was.

"I... didn't," said Paul, sounding as though he had first checked himself to make sure.

"Me neither," Greg said. "But, ugh, someone did."

The two cousins turned to me, their shirts pulled up over mouths and noses, hoping they'd serve as suitable gas masks.

"Don't look at me," I said, holding my hands up.

Dave sat motionless, staring at the floor.

Bobby's ensuing laughter and ridicule was relentless.

To say the ride home was an unpleasant one would be an understatement. Dave silently endured Bobby's continual indignities; the rest of us fought for room at the open windows. The smell of burning wood and leaves from some nearby brush fire overcame us, to our great relief. There seemed to be enough distractions to take our minds off the question most of us had, though: who or what was that on the quarry road?

When Bobby's car pulled up in front of his house, we couldn't exit fast enough. You'd think a bomb was about to go off, though I guess in some sense one already had.

"My god, McGrath. You're such a pussy," Bobby carried on. "And you *reek*. I better not have to clean my fucking back seat!"

I quickly changed the subject. "Who the hell was that back there?"

Dave was already halfway back to his house, with the unmistakable gait of someone with full pants.

"Who was that?" Bobby replied. "Who do you think it was, a giant wizard? It was the Grim-fucking-Reaper, dude, who else?"

"No, really," said Paul. "Was it one of your wicked-big college friends?"

"Seriously?" Bobby asked. "Out in the middle of nowhere. Near the quarry. In the dark. Just to scare you 'tards? Please." He exhaled smoke while he chortled. With an impressive flick, he shot his spent cigarette butt, sailing it thirty or forty feet down the road.

"He's out there late at night," Bobby continued. "Every night. You dorks never see him because you're too chicken-shit to go out there. Probably a good thing, though. You get too close, they say he brings that sickle down and *BAM!* You're done. Right in half.

He throws your bloody body parts down into the quarry. You sink down to the bottom and nobody ever finds you."

To that, no one spoke. We stood around in silence for a bit, probably to let what Bobby said sink in as he flipped his lighter open on his jeans, then struck it lit for the Salem already hanging from his lips.

"Hey, Ken," John called out to me. "You'd better hurry up and catch up to your boyfriend. He might need his butt wiped!"

"Ha. Ha. Screw you," I said as the others burst into laughter. I had to hold back from laughing myself. While Dave was by no means my best friend, he may have considered me his, and so I felt a friendly obligation to check on him. His situation was funny—at least to the rest of us—but at the same time I felt bad for the kid. As far as I knew, I was his only friend.

Mr. McGrath greeted me at the door. "Hey, Kenny. You guys all right? Get in a fight or something? Dave just ran upstairs without saying anything. It wasn't the Ward kid again, was it?"

"Uh, sorta," I said, entering the front door. "He and his brother drove a bunch of us out to see something near the quarry, trying to scare us. It scared Dave more than usual, I guess."

"Hm. The quarry, huh?"

The embarrassment was still cooling on Dave's cheeks when he came down the stairs, wearing fresh clothes.

"Oh, hey," he said, eyes darting between his father and me. "I, uh... I've got IBS, so... that kinda thing happens sometimes."

"Okay," I said. I had no idea what IBS was, but if it was what made the topic drop, I was happy just to let it end with that.

"Bobby Ward took you two out to the quarry tonight?" Mr. McGrath asked Dave.

Dave's eyes scanned the floor. "Yeah."

"And you two have never been out there at night before?"

"No," we both said.

"Hm. So you hadn't seen the Grim Reaper before, then."

Our two sets of teenage eyeballs became fixed on Mr. Mc-Grath.

"Wait," Dave said, holding his hand up. His pinkish cheeks reddened, though now from outrage rather than humiliation. "You know about that guy out there? Why'd you never tell me about him before?"

Mr. McGrath took a seat on the foyer stairs. "You know I don't like you kids—any kids—going out to the quarry at all, never mind when it's dark. Too many accidents over there. I know some people who've died out there. Always the stupid jocks. I didn't think I had to worry about you going out there at night until you were old enough to drive. I guess that's changed now, huh?"

Neither one of us answered. Mr. McGrath took a moment to consider where to begin.

"I was a bit younger than you two when I first saw him, scared the shi—uh, crap out of me. Bobby's father—Mr. Ward—he was actually with me at the time. This was before he became such a pain in the butt neighbor-from-Hell, and we were, believe it or not, friends.

"The quarry was actually functioning at the time, so the only people going out there were stone cutters. Construction workers. There was nobody going there to swim. Adam—Mr. Ward—had an older brother, Richie. Richie had this incredible car—a '52 Olds Super 88. Always kept that thing immaculate. Anyway, Richie would race people at night for money all the time. Adam and I knew about it, but we never knew when it was happening. But we really wanted to see him race.

"One night, Adam rides over to my house and wakes me up, tells me he overheard his brother talking about a race he was doing on the other side of Peasley, near Eastboro. We thought, 'Finally, now's our chance.' We'd heard that the quickest way to get to Eastboro was through a path by the quarry, but we'd never been out that way before. It didn't matter. We got on our bikes and we pedaled our butts off, in the dark, down that long, gravelly quarry road. No houses. No lights. Nothing. Just the sound of two kids huffing and puffing, bike chains rattling.

"We get to where we can barely see the outline of some of the machines and buildings up ahead. And that's when I saw it. I could see this huge, cloaked figure by the side of the road, across from the quarry pit, along the woods. I stopped dead in my tracks. Adam nearly ran right into me. He saw it too. This huge guy, just... standing there. We watched for maybe five minutes, just watching him. Adam wanted to turn back, but I was pretty determined to see the race. So I got back on my bike and started pedaling. The one gear my bike had couldn't keep up with how fast my legs moved. I could hear Adam behind me, scared half to death. Just as we're about to pass that giant at the edge of the road, BAM!"

"What?" Dave asked.

"I hit a patch of loose gravel. Went right down and skinned my left palm nearly to the bone. Adam, that no-good coward... he just kept on pedaling. Left me alone. I was out-of-my-mind scared. And then I looked up."

"Who was it? What did you see?" I couldn't get the questions out fast enough. Mr. McGrath leaned in.

"No one."

Dave said, "Wait, what are you talking about, 'no one'?"

"I mean no one," his father said. "It was just an enormous tree."

Dave's head flung back. "A fucking tree?"

"Hey!" Mr. McGrath said. "Yes, a tree. That big, hulking guy along the side of the road isn't a guy at all—just an old, rotten, hollowed-out tree."

Dave's father continued his story, about how the "Grim Reaper tree" had already been a sort of right-of-passage for newly licensed teen drivers for years, before he and Adam Ward happened upon it. The tradition eventually tapered off, then seemed to resurface in recent years, likely once Mr. Ward introduced the old tradition to his son. A sadist like Bobby Ward no doubt cherished the opportunity to christen kids to the Grim Reaper.

It was getting late. I said my good nights and pedaled home in the dark. Though I now knew that the thing we'd seen earlier was a tree, and though I was nowhere near the quarry, I kept to the center of the roads, far away from the bordering woods.

I beat my personal best time on the route home that night by ten minutes.

The rest of that summer was more of the same: hot, dry, and painfully uneventful. In August, the McGraths helped Dave spring for a barely working, piss-yellow '76 Chevette. Its floorboards were so rusted through that Fred Flintstone could've started it. Its engine begged for being rebuilt or, more appropriately, being put out of its misery. Dave was desperate to push the car past state inspection and spent the remainder of vacation with his lanky frame working underneath that shitbox.

Bobby Ward gave Dave some respite from further ridicule, thanks only to Bobby somehow landing himself a girlfriend, something I wouldn't have ever believed possible if I hadn't seen the delusional girl for myself. There was no more talk of that night in Bobby's car or of Dave's IBS, thank the good lord. And there was no more talk about the Grim Reaper tree.

When September and the new school year rolled around, so did basketball practice. And so did Bobby Ward. He slouched in the gymnasium stands during the first day of practice, switching from picking his teeth to repeatedly flicking his lighter open and closed with an echoing "click-snap," usually timed for when a player attempted a foul-line shot. With the more tolerable fall weather, he once again stuffed himself into his Peasley varsity jacket, completing his usual picture of despicableness.

Dave McGrath took the line for free-throw practice. He dribbled the ball three times and took position for his shot.

Clink-snap!

Dave released the ball in what was much more a straight line than an arc. The echo of Bobby's lighter was interrupted by the thud of Dave's brick shot against the backboard.

Bobby catcalled from the stands. "Briiick!" His girlfriend giggled in response.

"Keep it shut up there, Ward," Coach Hancock called out.

Dave took another ball and did his best to ignore the distractions from the stands.

Clink-snap! Clink-snap!

Dave's shot sailed in a perfect arc toward the basket, though that was the only thing perfect about it. The ball angled downward and well short of the rim of the hoop by at least six inches.

"McGraaath!" Bobby called out, mixed with his usual brand of cackling. "McGrath the giraffe! Air ball!"

"Shut up, Bobby, you fat piece of shit!" Dave yelled through clenched teeth. Only the sound of the air ball's final bounces killed the ensuing silence, as if to trail Dave's uncharacteristic outburst with an audible ellipsis.

"Or, what, McGrath?" Bobby finally chimed in. "You gonna crap in my car again? Hey, everyone, McGrath the giraffe crapped his pants in my car last summer! He was so scared he shat himself! It's true! Ask Kenny!"

"All right, you two, button it up!" screamed Hancock.

"Tell 'em, Ken," said Bobby. "You were there."

"Ward!" the coach interrupted. "Out of here! Now!"

As Bobby grabbed his girlfriend's arm to walk out, the eyes of everyone else were on me.

I am a horrible liar. My father used to tell me that if aliens ever landed on Earth and I had to convincingly lie to them in order to save all humanity from enslavement, we'd all be polishing flying saucers before two words passed my lips. Not that being able to easily determine whether I was lying or not was a bad thing to my father, mind you. If I can't find a way out of answering a question where lying is in the best interest of either myself or someone else I'm close to, my mouth resorts to stammering and my eyes will drift anywhere other than straight ahead.

I let my shrugging shoulders do the talking this time. Sometimes silence is the only safe way to lie.

I lived only about a mile away from the high school, so most nights after practice I usually hoofed it home rather than wait for my parents or someone else to give me a ride. That night, after I got about a quarter of a mile away from the gymnasium parking lot, headlights approached behind me, attached to a car with a muffler so loud that one might have thought an airplane was bearing down on me. The sound slowed as the car pulled up beside me. Slowing down and matching my walking speed, on my right, was Dave Mc-Grath, sitting behind what could barely be called an automobile. A Frankenstein's monster of machinery, its creator at the controls.

"Hey!" Dave called out from the open window of his res-urrected Chevette. It was now more Bondo grey than yellow. He spoke up more than usual, to be heard above the growling, hole-riddled muffler.

"Passed inspection?" I called back.

"It passed *my* inspection," Dave said, pulling the car to a stop. "Come on, I'll give you a ride."

Against my better judgement, I walked around to the other side of the car and got in. Thankfully the floor was intact, or at least the new floor mats provided a convincing cover-up job. Dave struggled with the shifter as he threw it into gear and brought the accelerator down hard, filling the air once again with muffler racket, joined with the acrid smell of spent, cheap fuel.

"Thanks," I said as we made our way up the road. "Listen, I'm sorry about that in there, I—"

"Yeah, no problem," Dave interrupted, brushing off the rest of my sentence. "I've got another thing I have to do first."

"O... kay?"

"That piece of shit Bobby Ward. I'm gonna make him know what it feels like to shit his pants. Right now. Tonight."

"How... ?"

"I'll tell you in a minute. Roll down your window."

We'd come to a stop light, and as I cranked the squeaky window down and thought to myself how bad of an idea it sounded to fuck with Bobby Ward, a familiar sound flooded the air and joined that of Dave's car: Bobby Ward's Camaro.

"Hey!" Dave called across from me. "Hey, Ward!"

Bobby's head snapped to look, and his eyes burned holes through the both of us. He rolled his window down. "The hell you want, McGrath?"

"I wanna see that Grim Reaper again. Meet me there in an hour."

Bobby's girlfriend joined him in an uproar of laughter. "What, so you can crap yourself again?" he said.

"Just meet me there. You'll see."

Bobby eyed us suspiciously for a moment while the light turned green. "Okay. All right. I'll meet you there. I've gotta hand it to you, McGrath, I didn't think you'd have the balls to go out there again. We'll see if you can control yourself this time. See you in an hour, pussies."

At that, the Camaro took off ahead of us before Dave could put his own car in gear.

"Um. Well, now what?" I asked.

Dave made no answer. Instead of heading straight ahead and toward home, Dave turned left, toward the quarry road.

When we pulled off the paved road and onto the leaf-covered gravel path, I couldn't let Dave's silence sit for another moment.

"Hey, what's the deal?"

Dave stopped the car. "Get out."

"Wait. What? Get out? Here?"

"All right, here's the plan. You'll stay here and wait for Bobby to show up. When he does, you jump around and wave your arms, panicking. You tell him I wimped out, kicked you out, and went home."

"And… ?"

"And he'll pick you up and take you with him, because he doesn't hate you like he hates me. And when you guys show up, I'll be hiding inside the hollow tree. I'll move it around, make some creepy noises. You start that whole yelling bit he does. He will freak the fuck out!"

"You think that'll work?"

"Yeah. Well, probably. Don't worry. Trust me, I'll be convincing. Later, you can tell me all about his reaction."

The plan sounded funny, I'll admit, but I knew Dave would have to be incredibly convincing to scare that lout Bobby Ward. He already knew that the Grim Reaper was nothing more than an old tree, so seeing it move around was more likely to get him curious than scared. But I was up for seeing how it would play out.

With an outburst of screaming metal, my door flew open upon its rusty hinges. I exited the car, and Dave drove away, sputtering into the dark. The usual under-tire crunch and pop of crushed stone became instead a white noise of crumbling, dead foliage that swept out in waves from beneath the car's undercarriage.

I didn't have to wait in the dark for long. Five minutes later, the rumble of Bobby Ward's car approached the quarry road. I immediately started waving my hands over my head and jumping, blinded by the Camaro's high-beams.

"Kenny? What the fuck?"

"Dave chickened out, man! He got pissed because I laughed, then he kicked me out. Can I get a ride?"

Bobby bellowed with laughter. "I knew it. What a pussy. Whatever. Get in."

Bobby's girlfriend sat next to him, so I climbed into the back seat.

"Hey, can we still go see the Grim Reaper?" I asked.

"Seriously? Man, you've got balls, Kenny. Not like your buddy the giraffe! All right, let's go. Marie hasn't see him yet."

A few minutes later, just before where we'd stopped on my first trip to this same place in August, I saw the Grim Reaper. I started into my act before Bobby could.

"HE'S THERE! OHMYGOD, HE'S MOVING! LOOK!"

Bobby glided the car a few feet more before hitting the brakes.

"He's what?" Bobby asked. "Did you say moving? Are you high, Kenny? It's not moving."

But Bobby was right. The tree was not moving. It remained as still as it had before, with only a few tricks of light to give the appearance that a cloak billowed about in the wind.

"No, no. Look! He's... he's moving! Listen! He's yelling or something!"

Bobby cut the engine and rolled his window down. The only sounds that greeted us were the *ting ting* of a cooling engine and the skitter of blown-about leaves.

Bobby chuckled. "Kenny, you asshole. Are you seriously trying to fuck with me? Really?"

Bobby started the car back up and pulled up to within twenty feet of the towering Grim Reaper. At that distance, it was plain to see the truth of what it was. A familiar wind sent the overhanging branches into a frenzy, sending shadows once again into a dance among the Reaper's cloak of rotted bark.

Bobby exited the car and strutted over to within a few feet of the Reaper. Even at Bobby's six-foot height, the decaying thing rose another two feet above him, seeming to stare above his head and into the darkness beyond the quarry. Bobby pulled his Zippo and a cigarette from his letter jacket pocket.

"Here! Now you see, guys!" he called out, laughing and turning toward us. "It's just a dumb, old, rotten stump! That's all it is! McGrath giraffe is scared shitless... of a stupid. Fucking. Tree!"

He struck the lighter open. *Clink-chick!*

Something happened then: the Grim Reaper—the hulking husk of what looked to have once been a mighty oak of Peasley Town Forest—began to move.

I was speechless at how realistic it looked, at how well Dave was playing the part. The branches that hung by its sides began to rise, shedding dead leaves and reaching upward and outward toward the unknowing Bobby. I had no time to go back into my act before Bobby's girlfriend started into a frenzy of her own.

"Oh my God! Bobby! He's right! That thing is moving!"

Bobby had little time to react. He lit the end of the cigarette dangling from his mouth. He was just able to mumble an annoyed "what?" out of his pursed lips before everything went to hell.

The branches moved quickly. Like giant tendrils, they extended and seized Bobby around his chest, then lifted the fat oaf from the ground. Marie shrieked. My jaw dropped. It wasn't possible for a skinny guy like Dave to do this. There was no way in hell.

Bobby struggled to break himself free, but it seemed his thrashing only got himself further caught up in the vines that entangled the branches.

"Wha—What the fuck?! Let the fuck go of me!"

The branches only pulled Bobby in tighter. In the midst of it all, the two became enveloped in a sudden eerie fog that materialized out of nowhere. I pulled myself together and got out of the car, if for nothing more than to make a run for it. But that wasn't fog.

It was smoke.

While Bobby tussled amongst a mass of branches and knotted vines, he'd dropped the lit Zippo onto the ground, into the piles of dry leaves at the base of the Reaper. Flames began to lick the bottoms of Bobby's feet as he remained embraced in the tree-branch hug.

"Dave! Dave, if you're in there, get out, man! The woods are on fire!" I yelled.

Bobby's eyes widened. "Dave? McGrath?! You mother fucker! I'll get you! I'll fuck you both!"

But there was no letting go. The branches held fast and only seemed to further tighten with every struggle Bobby made. His face reddened with a mix of range and panic, the fire continuing to grow around them.

"Dave!" I yelled again. "Give it up, Dave! Let's go!"

The engine of Bobby's Camaro thundered, and gravel and leaves left from under it as it backed away from the scene. Marie had taken the wheel. She spun the car around, nearly sending it off into the woods before punching it forward and speeding away down the road. With the car gone, the only sound now was that of crackling brush and Bobby's strained grunts. Then a voice.

"Wh—What the hell happened?"

It was Dave. He approached behind me, coming out of the forest, his eyes wider than my own. I could say nothing.

A sound came of rotten wood cracking, and I turned back to look just as whatever thing the Grim Reaper really was uprooted itself. Like no noise I'd ever heard before, the thing let out what I can only describe as a growl of something ancient and angry, a throaty animal roar that spoke of both torment and fury. Fire draped the entangled two as the ungodly shape lumbered across the ground and toward the deep quarry's edge. As the flames climbed Bobby Ward's jeans and began to ignite his corduroy jacket, he screamed. He screamed as one screams not of pain but of pure terror.

Both the roar and the screams died off as a distant echo, as the two tumbled sideways, falling into the quarry and out of sight.

DOUBLEBREAK

That was not the last we saw of Bobby Ward.

Bobby's girlfriend Marie eventually returned with police and fire vehicles in tow. While the fire became contained, an officer began asking us of Bobby's whereabouts. Marie hadn't seen all of what had happened. It was up to me and Dave to tell.

I started to explain. "He—"

"I was messing around with him and we got caught up in some trees," Dave interrupted. "Then he dropped his lighter. I got out of there, but... Bobby panicked and jumped into the quarry to put himself out."

Before we were asked anything more, another officer called out from the quarry. "We've got something down here!"

Ambulances were called in, and we saw what had been found. Bobby Ward, barely recognizable. He'd become a twisted mass of scorched, blackened and bloodied skin, naked but for a fragment of his jacket, the letter "P" of Peasley High, adhered to his chest within overlapping, melted skin.

The official assessment of Bobby's death was severe burns and drowning. An accident.

Dave's crappy car had broken down that night, far past the quarry. He'd never been able to execute his plan to become the Grim Reaper, to scare Bobby Ward into shitting his own pants. To this day I'm betting Dave still wonders to himself: did all that really happen? Was it all just some fucked-up dream? Because I know I do.

Why else would the Grim Reaper still be standing there today?

TEN-TWENTY

Speaking for myself, I am solemnly content carrying on about the halls and grounds of Saint Ambrose recalling the sweet and sordid tales of its populace. That, and perhaps telling of them to others like you, I suppose. I have need for nothing more. As it is, boredom has nary a place within my vernacular. I am unique in this quality, I do understand. One cannot, however, underestimate the actions of the disinterested, particularly those at a more youthful age.

Technology has presented options to those seeking escape from doldrum. Whether or not they choose to make appropriate use of these things remains in the hands and minds of their operators. Computers. The internet. Social media. And before these, citizen band radio. All a means of shouting into the virtual void for attention and, in some instances, interaction.

Communication takes on a whole new meaning once the virtual world meets physical, where the coming together, face-to-face, is what remains to make the connection true. A meeting is arranged. On computers, a pin is set and shared on a digital map. On CB radios, one merely needed to preface their present location to the other with a special code: ten-twenty.

"Breaker one-nine, breaker one-nine." *BOOLEEP.*

Nothing.

"Breaker one-nine. Anyone copy?" *BOOLEEP.*

Glen took a swipe at my hand as I attempted to key up the base station radio mic once more.

"Give it up," he belched. "You lost another one, man." He crumpled his empty can of MGD onto the table and left it to sit with the growing mountain of other fallen soldiers.

This was our Saturday night. This was just about every Saturday night for the entirety of our latter teen years. Nowhere to go. Nothing to do. No one else to talk to, really. Unless you counted Glen's smart-ass twin sister, Marie, which I did not. And, of course, anyone listening on the CB airwaves.

Glen and I were the epitome of introversion. As much as we bellyached about wishing we knew of a party to crash every weekend, we'd inevitably find some excuse for why a night in Glen's basement with a lukewarm case of beer was a much more preferable plan. Of course, a pair of pubescent boys with nothing but a CB radio and a pre-internet computer at hand are going to use MacGyver-like ingenuity to turn that seemingly harmless circuitry to entertaining use. And for a couple of dumbass troublemakers like us, I'm not talking about pulling another Jobs and Woz.

Believe it or not, it was indeed possible to meet girls with a CB. Well, "meet" is not quite accurate. I can't say what any of them looked like, mind you, but remember: we were horny teenagers with an absurd level of imagination when it came to visualizing women. And we weren't alone. Any rare time a girl's voice sounded in-channel, you had five, ten guys keying over each other to talk like unruly kids in a classroom. The key was finding the right time and place, then hope you had something cool enough to say to keep the conversation your own, usually taking it to a more private channel where the talk is less likely to get hijacked.

What did we talk about? The usual bullshit, I guess. It never got to sex talk, if that's what you're wondering. I'm sure we wished it had. Mostly we described what we looked like, each time with a growing amount of embellishment on both sides, I'm sure. What were our likes and dislikes, where we went to school. What we were up to at that moment, usually with lies like "working out" on our side.

Eventually, good nights would be said and radios would be silenced. It wasn't often we'd hear from the same girl again. Likely they were bored one night and hopped on their dad's radio for a laugh. For them, the airwaves was not a place to hang out, and not with the likes of losers like us.

We didn't always troll the airwaves for girls. Sometimes we just wanted to shoot the shit with anyone. More times than I can count, we'd pull pranks. It was virtually anonymous, after all. Glen not only had the massive base station radio in his basement, he had one wired up in the family van. The antenna he'd installed was so goddamn tall, we'd find ourselves removing it anytime we entered a parking garage.

Channel nineteen—or, as CB'ers call it, "one-nine"—was at least known in the day as the highway channel. For the most part, it was the go-to channel for truckers and the like, though people looking for road assistance would hop on there as well. It made sense: their best chance for help might be a passing truck hearing their call.

Channel nine was the one meant for emergencies, though it wasn't quite teeming with emergency crews at the ready. This was before the abundance of cellphones, mind you. But every now and then, one of us commoners would hop on one-nine and at least initiate a conversation with someone, then carry it on to a different channel, else hear the onslaught of angry, tired trucker curses.

One-nine was where I'd first heard Jo-Jo Baby. That was her handle; I never got her real name. Probably Jody or something. She only knew me by mine: Blue Thunder. Glen and I—well, mostly I—talked with her well into the previous Saturday night. It was going well, or so I thought. We'd moved the talk over to channel seven. Tonight she wasn't there. After a good couple of hours calling out on one-nine, it was clear she wasn't there, either.

I pushed the mic aside and drained the last dregs from my beer. Glen, ever ready with a reload, handed me another.

"All right, so what now?" I said. "Maybe we should head out for once."

"Can't. Fucking Marie's got the van tonight."

As though to add insult to injury, the basement door flew open, and there she stood.

"Fork over the keys, Dumbo. Are you... ? Oh my god, Dad is going to kill you if he knows you guys are down here drinking."

"Uh. No. Who do you think bought it for us?" Glen pulled the van key from his pocket and tossed it to his sister.

Marie sighed. "Look at you two. Is that all you're going to do all night? Sit there and talk to weirdos on the radio?"

"Not like we can go anywhere," said Glen. "The van?"

"Like that would matter," she said.

Glen shrugged.

"Fine. I'll tell you what. I can bring you and Sean to Sully's party. I just need to pick up Jill."

"Sully?" Glen said, irritated. He patted the half-empty case of beer. "He's a dick. We've got a better party here, thanks."

I gave him an incredulous look. "Dude, we—"

"Breaker one-nine, breaker one-nine," the radio interrupted. "Sledgehammer for Dumbo. Dumbo, you copy? Over."

Marie snickered. "Sheah, okay. Party hardy, 'tardies."

Glen threw an empty can in her direction. It clanged against the door as she left. "Wench." He rolled his chair closer to the CB and pulled the mic close. "Hey, Sledge. Dumbo. I copy. Let's take it to one-five." *BOOLEEP.*

"Can't you please turn that damned base-station 'boo-leep' shit off and say 'over' like the rest of us? Man. All right, catch you on one-five. OVER."

Sledgehammer was one of a few other guys we knew with a radio, better known to us off the air as Walt Bowden. He and Glen were known for monopolizing a channel for hours, ranting together about anything from girls uninterested in them to which was the superior radio antenna. Sometimes I'd chime in. But not this time. This time, I'd rather be at Sully's party. I'd rather be talking to Jo-Jo. Instead, I half-listened to Glen and Walt as I proceeded to polish off the better half of that case.

Between about my seventh and eighth beer, and in the middle of my friends' mind-numbing argument concerning radios using quartz crystals versus ICs: "Breaker one-five. Is that you, Dumbo? Over," a female voice said.

"Oh, you don't want to be speaking with that lame-o," said Walt. "He'll only talk your ears off over shitty nerd stuff all night while he's drinking shittier beer. Over."

"Sledgehammer only wishes he had beer at all. Who's this?" *BOOLEEP.*

For about ten seconds, there was no response.

"See, you put her to sleep already," came Walt's voice. "I bet you even made Blue zonk out on your floor."

I quickly shut my eyes and hung my tongue out of my mouth before Glen turned around to look. An empty can bounced close to my face. "Whoa! Hey!"

"Hey, Dumbo. This is Sassy Kitten. Over." The music from an unidentifiable boy band poisoned the background as she spoke.

"Who the hell's Sassy Kitten?" I asked, sitting up. Glen shook his head with a shrug, as if to say, "Who gives a shit? It's a girl, dumbass."

"Hey there, Sassy. Where do I know you from?" *BOOLEEP.*

"Well, you know I can't say my real name on here, but we go to school together. And... my girlfriend thinks you're hot."

I laughed. "She's gotta be talking about the cartoon elephant!"

"Oh you... Fuck off."

"What are you doing right now?" she asked. "Over."

"Uh, me and my buddy Blue Thunder are, y'know, lifting. Working out. Got us some beers. Uh, working out and drinking. Y'know." *BOOLEEP.*

"Girl, you don't have a chance," Walt interrupted. "Those two geeks are a match made in heaven. Nothing comes between those lovers. You wanna hook up? Talk to the Sledgehammer. That's me. Over."

"Fucking Walt," Glen muttered under his breath to the room.

"So are you guys up for partying? Y'know, after your workout? You can hook up with my girlfriend and... I can hook up with Blue Thunder. Over."

"Hell yes!" I said. "Tell her yes!"

"Um... no car?"

"Who gives a shit? We'll figure something out. Just go! Tell her yes!"

"Yeah, we're up for partying," Glen said into the mic. "What's your ten-twenty?" *BOOLEEP.*

Preceding a barrage of humiliating, seemingly incessant, girly laughter was the reply, now from a more familiar voice: "I'm... in your perverted dreams, Dum-BO!"

For several seconds, the channel was silent. Walt broke in laughing, mid-roar. "Dumbo! Burned!"

"Fuck-ing Marie!" Glen yelled to the room.

"Glen—I mean Dumbo—you really are dumb," Glen's sister said. All the while, more boy band music played in the background, intermixed with another girl's guffaws. "Seriously? Working out? Yeah, maybe your right hand!"

"You are so dead when you get home, Marie!" *BOOLEEP.*

"Yeah. Okay, What-ever. You and Blue Balls go and have fun 'working out.' Over and out!"

I fell back onto my ass, dropping my chin to my chest, not so much feeling defeated as I was humiliated. It served to remind me that more likely than not, people using CBs to meet people are impostors. Glen, Walt, and I were no different. Marie just chose to be a lot more up front about it. None of that seemed to stop me from clinging onto hope, that there were genuinely honest people out there to talk to and perhaps even meet someday.

I managed to get over myself and left the room to hit the head. When I got back, Glen was no longer talking with Walt. Instead, he was slowly turning through the CB's forty channels, coming up with not much more than static.

"Come on, dude, can we go do something else?" I said. "TV? Anything?"

Glen's response was interrupted by a sound from the CB, once its dial hit upon channel fifteen.

"—five. Breaker one-five. Over."

The signal was choppy, likely somewhat distant. The voice sounded abused, deep and tired, hoarse from likely too many cigarettes, too much booze, or both.

"Breaker one-five. Over," came the voice again. No response.

A sinister smile then grew on Glen's face before he cleared his throat and keyed the mic.

"Aw come on, man, don't do it," I said, knowing what he intended to do. "Not this guy."

"Sorry, but y'know, Marie set me off, dude. And maybe I just wanna balance the scales with this poor slob since she's not around."

"Go ahead breaker." *BOOLEEP*. He did his best to sound like a woman, and damn it all if he wasn't convincing. I'd heard him do this before, only it'd been to prank lonely, teenage boys, not some gruff trucker who'd sooner plug a steel-toe in your ass than sulk the whole thing off.

"Hey there, darling. What's your twenty? Over."

"Oh, wouldn't you like to know. What's your handle, cutie?" *BOOLEEP*.

"This is Big Guy. Who are you, honey? Over."

"Oooh, I like that! Big Guy. So... manly." *BOOLEEP*.

Glen let out a cackle and took a pull on his beer. I only shook my head and smirked. That was Glen being Glen. Or, rather, Glen not being Glen.

"Your handle? Over."

"Tell him Jo-Jo Baby," I said. What the hell, right?

"This is Jo-Jo Baby." *BOOLEEP*.

Static. Glen and I exchanged looks.

"You there, Big Guy? Y'know, I could really use a good fuck tonight. You think you could help?" *BOOLEEP*.

Again, for a good, long minute, there was nothing. Glen shrugged. "All right," he said to the room. "I guess let's see what's on T—"

"You're not Jo-Jo Baby." The voice was now a lot less friendly and much clearer.

Glen slid back over to the mic. "That's what they call me, Big Guy." *BOOLEEP*.

"What's your twenty... Jo-Jo Baby? Over."

"Oh, I don't know if I'm ready for that, Big Guy. We just barely met. How about I come to you?" *BOOLEEP*.

"You. Who are you? Jo-Jo Baby? No. What... is your twenty? Over."

Glen's voice was shaky now. "Now behave, Big Guy, or I'll have to leave. You wouldn't want me to leave already, now, would you?" *BOOLEEP*.

The voice from the man known as Big Guy grew then from mild irritation to full-on, absolute, and honest rage. "WHAT. IS. YOUR. TWENTY! WHERE ARE YOU? I WILL GUT YOU! I'LL GUT YOUR FAMILY! I'LL—"

I reached over and quickly turned the CB's dial to a random channel, filling the room again with the sound of static.

"Jesus," Glen said. "What the hell was that?"

My stomach churned. "You never know who you're gonna meet on there, huh?"

"Hey. You okay? Don't let 'Big Guy' get to you, man. It was just some creep. Or not. We'll never know, right?"

He was right. We were all untraceable, only found and seen if we wanted to be. If you don't want to hear from someone, you change the channel. Or maybe you never turn the CB on again. Either way, you move on. Like I guessed the real Jo-Jo had done.

"Big Guy," Glen continued. "Probably more like Tiny Dick. Turn on the TV. I guess let's see what's on."

Best idea all night.

"Hello? ... Hello? Is anyone there?"

My eyes creaked open under eyelids like sandpaper. I pulled my arm out from under my cheek and checked my watch. About two-thirty. I had no idea how long I'd been out. Judging by the hangover already setting in, it'd been a while.

"Hello?"

I sat up. Glen was splayed out on the floor, his hands embracing the empty case like a bedtime snuggy. He always was a lightweight. In front of me, a large digital number eighteen glowed from the face of the CB.

"Anyone? Hello?"

"Shit." I fumbled for the mic.

"Y—yeah. Uh, this is Blue Thunder. I copy." *BOOLEEP.*

Someone calling for help? This was... rare. You'd occasionally catch a stranded motorist calling out for a tow truck on channel nine, but this... this sounded dire.

"Oh thank God! Please. Please, I need help."

"Have you tried channel nine? Police are sometimes monitoring there." *BOOLEEP.*

"Yes. But no one's answering. Please, can you help me?"

Why were there no authorities monitoring channel nine? Saturday night. Most likely they had DUIs to hand out and a multitude of parties to break up.

"Hello? Are you there?" came the woman's voice again.

"I'm here." *BOOLEEP*.

"Oh my god! Thank you, thank you! You have to help me."

"Glen!" I called out to the room. "Glen! Wake up! You gotta hear this!"

Out cold. I swung the chair around and gave him a kick. A low, loud, irritated groan followed.

"Aw! What the fuck, man?!"

"Dude, listen! There's some chick on here looking for help. This is nuts. Listen."

"Are you still there?" I called into the mic. "What's your handle?" *BOOLEEP*.

"My... my what? My name is Christine. Can you help me? Please!"

Glen kicked at my chair. "Oh, come on! Bull. Shit. She's on channel eighteen! It's gotta be Marie fucking with us again, dude!"

"Does that sound like Marie? Or Jill? She says she came up empty on nine. What the hell, right? Let's see how it plays out."

Glen shrugged and sat up.

"What's your twenty, Christine? I mean your 10-20. Your location." *BOOLEEP*.

"I'm broken down off I think exit seventeen somewhere. Off route 2A in Eastboro. I'm stopped near a sign for... Saint Ambrose-something."

"Eastboro?" Glen said. "Shit, she's probably stuck out in the middle of the state forest. That's the cemetery."

I asked, "Do you need us to call you a tow truck?" *BOOLEEP*.

"No, no. Please, I don't have any money and I just need somebody to come pick me up and take me home. Please, I'll... I'll do anything. I'm so scared."

Glen and I exchanged looks with our eyebrows peaked. "Hold on, Christine." *BOOLEEP.*

"What do you think?" I asked Glen.

He rubbed his hand under his sorry excuse for a beard. "Maybe it's legit. Maybe it's not. But it doesn't matter, right? 'Cuz we don't have wheels."

He was right about that. There wasn't really anything we could do. Call the cops? I don't think that ever occurred to us. Where was the heroism in that, after all? Even if we had the van, neither of us were in any condition to drive. We didn't have many options.

"Oh! I know!" Glen was now on his feet. He gave me a shot on the arm. "Sledge—Walt! We can have him pick us up, and we can all go check it out."

"It's almost three in the morning. He still on?"

"Worth a try."

"Christine? Hold on, okay? We'll be right back." *BOOLEEP.*

"Okay. Please hurry."

Glen took control of the radio, switching the channel to nineteen. "Breaker one-nine. Sledgehammer, you copy?" *BOOLEEP.*

"Yeah. What do you want, Dumbo? You still wanna argue your Realistic against my Cobra? Over."

"No, man. You need to come pick us up. We need to go check something out." *BOOLEEP.*

"Check what out? Over."

"Will you just come pick us up?" *BOOLEEP.*

"Not until you tell me what it is we're checking out. Over."

Glen looked at me, defeated. "Go to one-eight." *BOOLEEP.*

"Ohhh-kay. Roger."

Turning the radio back to eighteen, we caught Christine mid-sentence, sounding frantic. "—ou there? Dumbo? Hello?"

"Yeah, I'm back. Sledge, you here?" *BOOLEEP.*

"I'm here. Who're we talking to? Over."

"This is Christine. I really need someone to come help me. I'm stuck in the middle of nowhere and I'm scared."

"Before you ask, Sledge, she doesn't want cops or anything like that. She just wants someone to come pick her up. She's over in Eastboro." *BOOLEEP.*

"Well, I can do that. I'm only a few miles away. Over." I threw my head up and cursed at the ceiling.

Glen slammed his hand onto the mic's transmit button. "Sledge, take it back to the last channel." *BOOLEEP.*

Back on nineteen, Glen's tone grew more clearly annoyed. "Sledge? You there? Sledge!" *BOOLEEP.*

"Yeah, I'm here. What the hell's wrong with you? Over."

"Come pick us up, man." *BOOLEEP.*

"What? You're, like, miles out of the way. Why would I go and do that? Over."

"Just come pick us up." *BOOLEEP.*

Walt laughed. "What, you finally find a CB girlfriend and you're afraid I'll steal her? Won't... what's her name? Jo-Jo Baby? Or Wildflower or Jade Kisses? Won't they be jealous? Oh, right, you two bozos scared 'em away! You're a sorry bunch, the two of you."

The channel grew silent for a moment, while we stewed on Walt's words.

"This girl's looking for help, and so I'm gonna go help her. I'm heading back to one-eight," Walt said. "Over."

Of course, we followed.

"Breaker one-eight. You there... Christine? Over."

"Dumbo?"

"No, this is Sledgehammer. I'm close, so I'm gonna come help you out. Can you give me your twenty? Over."

"So... Dumbo's not coming?"

"Nah, he's too far out and doesn't have a car. I'll take you where you need to go. Over."

"Okay, um, I'm near a place called Saint Ambrose, off 2A. Um. Over."

"I know where that is. I'll be there in ten. Over."

The following ten minutes felt more like twenty, Glen and I spending most of it within the white noise of CB radio static.

"I heard Wildflower maybe moved to California," Glen mumbled, mostly to himself. "Jade was just... I dunno. Anyway, I barely talked to her."

Walt's voice broke in. "Christine? You copy? Over."

"Yes, I'm here."

"I'm passing the sign for Saint Ambrose. Where are you from here? Over."

"Just a little further. I see your headlights."

"Roger that. What the—"

For the next minute, there was nothing. Glen and I looked at each other, brows furrowed and jaws slack. Glen keyed the mic.

"Sledgehammer? You copy? What's going on?" *BOOLEEP.*

"Uh. Yeah, I'm here," Walt said, his voice sounding shaky. "Christine? You copy? Over." Again, silence.

"Sledge, what's going on?" *BOOLEEP.*

"There's... a truck out here. Like a big rig. This chick driving a truck? Where the hell is she?"

"No idea." *BOOLEEP.*

"Okay. Guess I'll go check it out. Be back on in five. Over."

Five minutes passed. Then ten. Twenty. Static. Only static.

"Sledge? You copy?" *BOOLEEP.*

Nothing. Thirty minutes. The door to the room crashed open. I almost pissed myself. Into the room poured Glen's sister, stinking of spent cigarettes and fruity liquor. Strawberry, maybe.

"Oh my god," Marie slurred. "You two are still trying to get laid on that thing?"

"Fuck off, Marie," Glen said.

"Whatever. Fine, I'm snacking, then crashing."

"Wait! Give me the van key."

"The what? The hell you want the keys now for? Party's way over."

"Come on. Just give 'em."

After several failed jabs at her coat for a pocket, she managed to slip her hand in and pull the key out. It clattered to the floor at her feet.

"Have at it," she said before stumbling up the stairs and sniggering like a stuffed-up wino. Glen got to his feet and snatched up the keys.

"Well?" he said. "Let's go."

The ride to Eastboro was a decent thirty minutes from Glen's house. Walt was right in not going out of his way to get us, if this girl Christine was really desperate for help. Throughout the entire ride, I took to using the van's CB to reach out for Walt, Christine... anyone on channel eighteen. No response. Not a soul. Even our old haunt, channel nineteen, had no one.

Glen slammed his hand onto the steering wheel. "Fucking Walt! The asshole probably turned his radio off."

"Why would he do that?"

"Who knows? It's Walt! Selfish-fucking-Walt."

Nothing was going on. I knew that. At least, I knew nothing was happening in the way Glen thought. If I'm being completely honest with myself, I knew nothing ever could or would happen between a closed-up loser like me and another stranger of the opposite sex, meeting anonymously on a CB radio on a weekend night. Or any night. But it made me feel good, even if just for an hour or two, or maybe over a couple of nights. And so what if they essentially disappeared after that? We both had our fun. Or at least I did. Both pretending to be someone we're not, someone we want to be or appear to be, at least when only a voice is to be heard and a story with a questionable degree of truth is to be told. And all of us were the same sort of loser. Glen. Walt. Me. All those girls we talked to. We were all the same. In the days before the internet, it wasn't silent words on a screen that gave us anonymity. For us, it was the airwaves, with only a voice to identify us by. That anonymity was at least something we could count on. What came from that voice was as believable as we wanted it to be.

At that hour on a Sunday morning, the roads were clear. An occasional delivery truck blew past heading the other direction. Glen turned the van onto the exit seventeen offramp, passing by only a few houses before plunging into the darkened state forest road. The cemetery, I knew, was under a mile ahead.

I called into the mic. "Breaker one-eight. Christine? Sledge-hammer? You copy? Over."

Glen slowed the van as it passed by the closed gates of Saint Ambrose. Walt's car was nowhere. No sign of his car, nor a truck. Beyond the ornate walls was complete blackness, but for the light from the windows of the chapel and mausoleum. *A late night for visiting dead loved ones*, I thought. Probably a priest preparing for visitors and mass later that morning.

"Drive a little further," I said. "There's a parking lot."

"Sean, he's not gonna be there. They took off."

"No! Look!"

Stopped in the middle of the parking lot was Walt's beat-up Monte. Exhaust till sputtered from its undercarriage as it idled, alone in the dark. Its driver-side door stood ajar, though the car's interior light was off. Beyond it were empty parking spaces and the bordering woods. No sign of other vehicles. No sign of anyone. No sign of Walt.

Glen stopped the van twenty yards from Walt's car. "Give him a shout. See if he's still in there."

"Sledge—Walt? You copy? This is Blue and Dumbo. We're behind you."

Outside, I could hear my own voice echo back to me in the distance. Walt's radio was still on, with the volume turned up.

Glen rolled his window down and called out. "Walt! Stop fucking around, man! Where's the girl?"

"Christine?" I said into the mic. "Christine, do you copy? What's your twenty? Over."

Glen stepped outside the van and slammed the door shut behind him with pissed-off force. "I've had enough of your know-it-all shit, Walt! Stop fucking around and come out!"

As Glen stormed away toward the idling car, Christine's voice came over the CB.

"I'm here, Dumbo. But don't worry. I'm okay." She giggled. It was a feminine, girlish laugh, one of mischief and sex, and felt as though to go on for minutes. As she continued to transmit, her voice gradually deepened, as the giggle transformed to that of a laugh much more sinister and masculine. From the van's CB, from Walt's. It was everywhere.

"Who the hell is that?" Glen called back to the van as he continued to make his way to Walt's car. I threw my hands up and shrugged. The man on the CB continued transmitting, never stopping for our response.

"You boys are disgusting, you know that? Carrying on with poor ladies in distress. Arguing about who's going to go and save the day because you think you... what? Might get a piece of ass for doing so? Pssh. Pathetic."

It was clear now who both voices belonged to: the man from channel fifteen, from earlier that night. The enraged lunatic who went by the handle of Big Guy.

"Glen!" I called out my open window. "It's that crazy nut ball from earlier!"

"Who?"

"That crazy dude: Big Guy. He's fucking with us, man! He sent us out here for nothing!"

"The real way to get anything from these girls, fellas, is the way I go about it," Big Guy continued. "They don't want some stuffed-up nerds in their mommy's basement drinking poppa's beer, with barely enough hair on their balls to call themselves men.

"They want someone... like me. They might not know it right away, but they catch on fast. Missy. Jennifer. Oh, sorry: Wildflower and Jade... Kisses, was it? Yeah, that was it."

Glen spun around. "What? Did he say something about Jade? What the hell?" He turned back to Walt's car, picking up his pace. "Walt! Come on, Bowden! This is all bullshit!"

"Joanne was another story. She... well, she really did have a thing for limp-dicked geeks. Jo-Jo... yeah, that was her. Seems you were on to something with that one, Blue. Had to convince her I was you in order for her to come out and meet me. 'Hi, Jo-Jo Baby. I think we should finally meet up. How about at the mall?' How about that? Was I convincing? Whatever. Not my best work. But it was enough for her."

I tried transmitting a reply. "Who is this? You are one sick fuck, you know that?" It was no use. He wasn't going to hear me, and his transmission was overpowering anything mobile. Unusual, even for a trucker's radio. This was base-station level. Big Guy had the comm, and he wasn't letting up.

I watched as Glen reached Walt's open door, then as he stumbled backward onto the pavement.

"You boys do pretty good impressions yourselves, you know. But you do a shitty Jo-Jo. She wasn't quite the slut you were making her out to be. But I had to be sure. Maybe she'd made it out of that dumpster? No. I knew that. But if there's one thing I hate more than loose ends, it's people FUCKING WITH ME!"

Glen was on his feet now, sprinting back to the van. He held a hand to his mouth, though all it did was delay what came forth onto the ground as he slammed against the driver-side door.

"It—It's Walt!" Glen said, catching his breath. "He's fucking strangled by his mic cord in there! His face is all fucking blue and... and his tongue... Holy shit! He's dead, man!"

"Wh—What?! Are you sure?"

"You must be wondering where I am right now," the radio bellowed. "You want to know my ten-twenty. Am I right? I was thinking the same thing about you, y'know. Trying to nail down just where in the hell you two pencil-necks were holed up. Your pally there... Sledgehammer, is it? He was kind enough to tell me.

Kinda had it stuck in his throat for a bit, so to speak, so I helped get it out of him."

Glen reached through the window and snatched the mic from my hand. "Fuck you! You sick fuck! You killed him! Why would you do that? You killed Walt! He's just a fucking kid!"

"Glen! He's still transmitting! He can't hear you!"

He ignored me. "Is there anyone there? Breaker one-eight! Breaker one-eight!"

Glen let go of the mic, and Big Guy picked up mid-sentence. "—would gut your family? Well, gosh. I was just messing with you. But, y'know... I hear that a SASSY little KITTEN around here could maybe use some company... now that I've taken poppa cat outside."

"Turn to channel nine!" I screamed. "We need to call the cops or something!"

"No. Wait. Sassy Kitten?" Glen said "Is that... Is he... Is he talking about... But he's not—"

"I do want to thank you boys for reminding me that it's time for me to relocate. I don't need your godforsaken backwoods towns. I sure as hell don't want 'em. It's time I embraced the new and say goodbye to the old, you know? Get myself... I dunno, a computer. Fuck this CB horse shit, having to deal with you dumbass punks. Then I can be anywhere. Am I right? Can be... from... anywhere. Miles... miles away. A CB... well, it can only carry you so far. Gots to be close to the source, right? And any pervert can listen in on the whole thing. Like now, right? Just like I know where you are... right now, Mister Dumbo. Like I know... you know, right now... MY TWENTY."

DOUBLEBREAK

BOOLEEP.

THE SADDLE

*S*aint Ambrose has had its fair share of, shall we say, unexpected visitors. Not unwelcome, mind you—everyone is free to enter the buildings and grounds, but only during our normal hours of operation, and solely for the purpose of visitation. Leaving flowers, trinkets of affection, perhaps more than a few tears: all permissible and within expectations.

Wandering onto the property after hours would be truly unwise for a multitude of reasons, much less so that of enduring the wrath of yours truly. Having the audacity to come here to steal, whether or not during visitation hours, well... may a higher being have mercy on their soul.

Alas, despite the fair warnings our signage proclaims, there are some desperate enough. Or foolish. Perhaps they work on behalf of external forces neither I nor they can comprehend, akin to a horse guided by an unseen hand into a place it does not belong, with the helpless rider strapped into the saddle.

Courage is being scared to death but saddling up anyway.

It was something Shawn used to say to Ruth when she was too scared or shy to do something she wanted—rather, needed to do. She's pretty sure he got the saying from someone famous, but the man loved horses, so she thought it a fitting phrase for him to latch onto. And she still thinks of it when she's too chickenshit to do what she wants to do—what she needs to do.

Sometimes courage has nothing to do with it at all. Sometimes it's flat-out self-preservation or common sense. And when those situations face you square on, you may as well take that cowboy saying and toss it right into the toilet, because no manner of courage makes up for being stupid.

Ruth had barely a recollection of how she got there, squatting below the beam of Rack's flashlight, picking at a mausoleum keyhole, thinking of Shawn. She hated Rack for bringing her there, but he was at least good at finding jobs worth paying a damn in that godforsaken armpit of the world, worth paying for head doctor bills that a cop's salary couldn't touch. She would have seen to it that Rack was sporting orange duds at Hillsborough County, or among the many laying prone just inside, if he wasn't at least good for that.

She winced as something flared within her brain, then stood, smacking her head on Rack's flashlight. "Shit! Why'd you pick this place?" she asked, rubbing her head. "*This* place."

Rack threw his hands up. "You picked it, remember? Said 'something-something Ambrose'... A big score. Biggest yet. Wouldn't say nothing else. Maybe you could, y'know, clue me in yourself?"

She shook her head. "No. No, I... How can I not remember that?"

"You better remember. We need this one. Damn place gives me the creeps. How much longer?"

"I dunno. Few more minutes. Now shut up."

The lock was popped five minutes ago, but Rack didn't know that. Ruth knelt once again and resumed picking at a keyhole that had already relented, like one would a toothpick digging at a stubborn gobbet. She wasn't ready to go in.

Saddle-on up, Ruthie.

"Right. Saddle-up," she whispered.

She supposed having courage had as much to do with it as stupidity after all. The fact that she still wore her uniform on jobs like these pointed her actions firmly toward the latter camp, but it helped serve as a cover story more than once.

The iron door opened without a sound into the darkness, into the cold, into where only death lay.

"Yesss. All right, ladies first."

"No. Go ahead."

Rack shrugged, lifted the toolbox, and shone his flashlight into the gloom. "Whatever you say. Officer."

She hated that Rack felt the need to say that. She could sense his wise-ass smirk as he stepped through the open doorway, as though what lay beyond was nothing at all. It was so easy for him to treat it as just another job, when the clothes he was wearing didn't serve as a contradiction to the task at hand. Her uniform was all part of the plan: she knew that. Always had been. It didn't make it feel any less violating.

"Good to be working with you again, Cassidy," Rack said. "Remember our last job? Shit, must've been a year now since—"

Since the last time I was here, she thought. *Saying goodbye.*

"Yeah, something like that."

Rack shrugged off the interruption and continued into the cold air of the mausoleum. Ruth followed close behind, her own flashlight lit. The scent of flowers for the dead stung her senses and rattled her already pounding head as she shut the door, echoing off the marble floor and placarded tombs. There was a feeling of finality, of no turning back. If only the proverbial horse she'd saddled onto would carry her forward.

"Jesus this place is big," Rack said, spinning around. "Must be a thousand of 'em."

"Twelve-hundred," she said.

"Really? Damn." He shone his flashlight along the marble vaults, its beam catching nameplates as it went. "All right, so... where is he?"

"Section 8C, row 28. Second from the bottom." It came to her unhindered, automatic.

She'd last been there so long ago yet recalled Shawn's resting place like one would a friend's phone number. Or a lover's. She tried to shake the thought away.

Rack flinched, fazed. "You remember it just like that?"

Her head continued to shake. "No. Forget it. Someone else."

Ruth turned her eyes to her left, toward Section 8C, where along row 28 and two doors up from the floor was a name plate she was sure she'd never cast eyes upon again. Yet there she was, mere footsteps away. And for what? Still, she wasn't sure, and Rack's patience with her would no doubt grow thin at the prospect of her not knowing.

"So. Lead the way," said Rack, with a flourish of his hand.

She scanned the names outside the tombs around her, stacked four high, floor-to-ceiling. Some were clearly older than others: their name plates more tarnished, vases empty of flowers or containing skeletal, leafless stems. Those more recent had flowers in varying states of decay or with trinkets and mementos placed at the foot of their stack: notes, toys, more flowers.

Shawn had a plastic Appaloosa under his, she recalled. She had left it then, before walking away for what should have been forever.

"Hey, Cassidy," Rack said.

The pain in Ruth's skull surged as she snapped out of her thought.

"What do you call these things we're looking at, on the graves? The things the names are on. Doors?"

"They're tombs. Graves are outside, in the ground."

"I think they're, like, seals or something. Can't call 'em doors, right? Ain't like anyone's opening them all the time, y'know? 'Cept us, I guess."

"Yeah. Well. Some doors are meant to stay shut."

"Not tonight they ain't. Not all of 'em."

What kind of job was it, really? Parting the overly wealthy, the exceedingly fortunate, of their over-abundances seemed an entirely different sort of job than relieving the dead of precious items left to rot alongside them. But was it so different? Were they not merely indulgences left to waste? Perhaps a more honorable thing was to see them do some good in the world than have them forever sealed away? Perhaps, she thought, that was reasoning enough to get her to find this "job," as loose as that term was for it. It still didn't put a veil over what kind of place it was, nor who took residence there.

If not Shawn, who was she looking for? She may have had a hand in putting some of the bodies there over the years, but names tended to wither away like the petals littering the floor. She chose to keep those names locked away in the mausoleum of her mind, with doors that are forever closed. Closed, perhaps, but apparently not sealed, with an occasional issuance that served to drive her mad.

"C'mon, Cassidy, which one?" Rack's tone bordered on annoyed. "Just blurt it out. Come on. First name that pops in your head. Tick-tock, tick-tock! Go!"

Shawn. No!

"The blacksmith's son," she said, though not knowing why. "The blacksmith's son. That's all I got."

"What? Blacksmith's son? That's not a name. That ain't gonna be on the front of any of these doors."

Ruth stepped forward, reading nameplates as she went.

"Maybe you're wrong," she said. "There's more than just names and dates on these."

"Yeah, all right. But 'blacksmith's son?' I dunno. Don't you have a name? Just need a name. C'mon, think. That's what you cops do."

What did he think she'd been doing the moment they'd arrived? And before that? And what did come before? She presumed a car ride, a phone call. All of that lost now, and none of it made sense.

"How did I tell you about this job?" she asked.

"What do you mean 'how?' You called me, remember?"

"No. What did I say? I didn't tell you a name or anything then?"

"Naw, you just said it was in Saint Ambrose's and it was enough of a score we'd be set for life." Rack averted Ruth's gaze. He suddenly didn't look so good. Her cop's intuition fired.

What are you not telling me? she wanted to say but was stopped short as Rack's flashlight flickered out. Ruth turned her own light toward Rack, but he had disappeared as fast as his light had gone dark. "Rack?"

Her flashlight sputtered out.

THUD! THUD! THUD!

The hairs on her neck and back sprung lives of their own, standing at shaky attention beneath her uniform. The pulse within her brain beat in rhythm to the reverberating sounds around her. She fought the urge to double over in pain as her hand flew to her sidearm.

"Rack?!"

THUD! THUD!

The sound of a match being struck, then a soft glow from her left.

"Hey," a male voice said.

She threw the latch off her weapon and drew it, wheeling about. It was not Rack.

The man stood twenty feet from Ruth at the center of the hallway. Along with the cigarette that hung sideways from his lips, the stained-glass-colored moonlight barely illuminated the contours of his pale face in the dark. He was young, well-dressed, and despite his submission with one hand raised, unafraid.

"I'm a cop," she said. "Who the hell are you? What are you doing in here? Put your other hand up!"

Slowly, he complied. "I know who you are, Officer Cassidy. Thought you'd be happy to see me."

Her pistol remained drawn and ready, safety released. There was nothing good about someone lurking in the dark of a place like that, no matter their business or intentions. She resisted the urge to call out to Rack again. She could explain a uniformed cop's presence just about anywhere, but not with her slime-ball partner-in-crime in tow.

"How the hell should I know who you are?" she asked. "I can barely see you."

He remained still, with only the movement of slender tendrils of smoke rising from his silhouette. An occasional auburn glow from a cigarette inhale gave hint to the bemused smile that held it. Something about it became at once somewhat familiar to Ruth, but only just.

"You work here?" she asked.

A drawn-out exhale. "Something like that, Ruthie."

A realization struck her, and she did all she could to stifle a cry.

"Sh-Shawn?" Ruth whispered.

At that, the man began lowering his hands.

"Keep your hands up!" Ruth yelled. "Wh-What the hell is going on? Who the fuck are you?"

"Ruthie," the voice said with calm reassurance. "Ruthie, it's me."

Ruth released the dead flashlight, letting it clatter to the floor, as she drew the now freed-up hand to steady the first. Her finger teased the safety on her pistol as she fought back tears.

"Shut up! He is dead! Shawn is dead! What kind of sick fuck are you, calling yourself Shawn, huh? Who are you?!"

The man dropped the cigarette, then took a careful step forward, into a shaft of moonlight that illuminated his face in full. Ruth's tears released.

"Hey, partner. Good to see you again."

Through a watery veil, Ruth saw that before her was indeed Shawn, just as she'd last seen him. It did nothing to make her lower her weapon; as much as such a vision brought her joy, innate intuition kept her in check.

"No," she said, shaking her head in disbelief. "No, no, no."

Shawn sighed. "I know. Sorry to drop in on you this way."

THUD!

Again, to Ruth's right. Again, her head. She snapped to and spun around, her gun now pointed in the direction of the sound.

"Rack?!" she called out.

"Rack's gone, Ruthie," said Shawn. "It's just you and me right now. He's not coming back."

"What do you mean 'right now?' Who else is coming? My dad?!"

Shawn chuckled nervously. "No, not your dad."

THUD!

"What the fuck is that?" she said. "What's going on?"

Shawn stepped closer. Ruth kept her gun pointed down the dark hallway, where lay what sounded like imminent threats. The man before her—the person who had to be Shawn but couldn't be—was no threat in that place. As her tears continued their descent, Shawn gently placed his hands on her shoulders.

"I'm sorry, Ruthie. I'm sorry I wasn't able to be there for you anymore."

He gently placed a hand to the back of her head, then into the light. Blood flowed from his fingers and glistened in the moonlight as it fell in large droplets to the floor.

Ruth resisted the urge to reach back, to search for a phantom wound she could not feel, that she would not let herself believe to be any more real than this man standing before her. To reach out for either of them meant to bring a reality to the nightmare: that her mind, like Shawn, was lost.

"It's why he was able to take you here," Shawn said.

"He?" she began today, before another round of *THUD! THUD! THUD!*

"He's coming. Ruthie. You have to remember now."

THUD!

Ruth jumped, her nerves shot. The sound was louder now, closer, more threatening.

"This is crazy. I really am going crazy. I-I-I don't know what you mean. Remember what? What is that? Who's coming?"

"Shhh. You're not crazy. The name, Ruthie. The one you came for. It's important."

THUD! THUD!

Ruth tried to adjust to the darkness down the seemingly never-ending hallway, from where the approaching sounds came.

Shawn turned Ruth to face him and put his hand on her wrist. She complied as he slowly helped her lower her gun.

"It's time to saddle up, Ruthie. Don't be afraid. Come on. You said something about a blacksmith."

"A... A what?"

"A blacksmith's son. "Son of a blacksmith. "Son...

"Son—"

"—of a bitch!" Shawn cursed, gagging, and barely able to keep his composure and late dinner down while facing the grizzly scene. His partner and girlfriend, Ruth, had seen much worse during the war, though that did little to help quell her reaction.

The officers' target stood before them, a mess of stress and sweat, blood and gore, the latter being much less his own and more that of the slain strewn across the floor. He didn't look up as he spoke, his head hanging low in a display of shame and bewilderment, face caked in maroon filth and his own hair. The boy in his teens stood behind the church altar, naked but for a pair of blood-soaked boxers. In one of his outstretched hands was a sword the likes of which might be seen possessed by a medieval barbarian, and just as bloody.

The boy's chest heaved as he stood otherwise motionless, facing the two officers. His victims—old churchgoers, Ruth's guess—were positioned in supplication before him, most sans heads or hands. The pools that had flowed from their missing limbs congealed along the floor at the boy's feet in a neat, shimmering pool. The stench of copper and the soiled garments of the dead was overwhelming.

"Kid!" Ruth called out, tears of strain blurring her vision. "Kid, put down the weapon. I don't want to have to drop you."

Her voice was steady, relaxed, her sidearm poised atop her outstretched hand. He was a kid, barely sixteen from what she could tell. So, no: though the horror he'd clearly unleashed was inhuman, she did not want to have to put a bullet in him. He was sick and, despite the grizzly scene, not completely removed from getting help, she hoped. Death wasn't yet his only option.

"I..." The teen's voice trailed off, as though he did not believe the next words that would leave his mouth.

"God dammit! Drop it!" Shawn commanded. He stood beside Ruth with a disposition much less sure.

"We're not gonna say it again," Ruth said. "Drop the sword. Now!"

The kid looked from one hand to the next, locking on the blade as though seeing it for the first time. As he did, he spoke in volume and intensity as if to an unseen audience of many.

"The hammer strives not to win wars, but to smother the fire of life!"

Ruth and Shawn shot each other a look. The boy went on.

"Smother... the fire of life."

"What the hell is this he's yelling about?" Shawn muttered from the side of his mouth. "We'll take him down on three."

"Shawn—"

"Look at this place," Shawn said. "Listen to him. Time to saddle up, Ruthie—there's no other way this can go."

"Only the nail!" the murderer continued ranting. "Only the nail the hammer seeks!"

With that, the boy set his sights on the only other living souls in the church. In one quick motion, he leaped from his position behind the altar. He was airborne but for a heartbeat before Ruth's bullet found its mark, and the boy crumpled back to the floor with only half of his head intact, the sword continuing forward, relinquished. Scattered bits of him littered the floor-to-ceiling stained-glass windows, bringing blues to purple, yellows to orange, and anything else to a deep, dark red.

The gunshot's report seemed to last an eternity. Ruth's finger remained fully depressed on the trigger. The air aromatic of sulfur and copper, of spent gunpowder and blood.

Ruth turned. Time slowed. She stared at her partner—her lover—and lowered her gun.

Her eyes left him and scanned over at the bodies surrounding the altar for what seemed like the first time. They were without rejoice or relief. Without judgment. Without life. And now joined by the one they'd been poised to worship and, too, Shawn, another reluctant addition to their gruesome flock.

The blade had sought and found its intended target. Shawn's head lay open upon the altar, split so evenly as to travel the length of his septum.

The silence of the moment ceased as the large blade that was lodged within her boyfriend's skull clattered to the thinly carpeted floor at her feet. With it, her troubled mind resumed its spiral downward, a direction she'd long sought to reverse with the help of professionals, and that Shawn had since displaced. Her sanity was no match for his absence.

Upon the center of the sword's guard, crossed hammers beside the face of a lion, blackened by ages of soot and blood. Below that, in intricate script, the name of its creator.

Ruth felt the world leave her as she fell to her knees. The chaos and static deranging her mind was joined but not interrupted by a sound familiar to her, but one she couldn't care less about then nor ever again.

"Officer Cassidy, do you copy?" the radio at her dead partner's side blared.

"We have an ID on the suspect. Name is Brian—"

"MacGowan."

Ruth's eyes widened and the flow of tears ceased, while a calmness began to wash over her. She realized then what she'd missed most about not having Shawn in her life: his reassurance that she could do no wrong, even when that was all she felt she ever did.

He also had a way of giving her a nudge when she needed it most.

"Right. MacGowan," Shawn said with relief. "Scottish. Son of the smith."

Ruth's world slowed as she dropped her gun and let herself fall into Shawn's arms.

"You did it, Ruthie," he whispered. "Way to saddle up, girl."

He held her there, saying nothing more.

She still had no idea why she was there, how Shawn was there, or why such a name was so important and so difficult to muster. All she cared for then was the unlikely reunion. To feel for once safe, and with a tortured mind finally at peace.

Retired Officer Ruth Cassidy remained sedated in the dirty laboratory bed, an array of sensors covering her wounded head. Doctor Roland hobbled over with his cane once again to the set of monitors, still displaying the computer-generated interior of the Saint Ambrose mausoleum.

THUD! THUD!

He cast a glance over at the woman in bed, puddles of sweat and tears soaking the sheets by her face. He turned the monitors off, retrieved a cellphone from beside them, and typed out a call.

"It's Roland. I finally got that name for you. 'MacGowan.' Yes, right. Yes, glad we didn't have to resort to, well, more dangerous means. She's lucky. A woman in her mental state, the brain damage... She might not have survived the next phase.

"Strange thing: it worked even when your avatar malfunctioned and blipped out of the simulation. The names in there didn't seem to matter. She just sort of told the name to... well, nobody. Just out of the blue.

"Anyway, payment's due tomorrow. Hope you find what you're looking for, Mr. Racksmith." The doctor ended the call.

Behind him, Ruth quietly saddled up and woke.

CONFIRMATION

It's a wonder to me sometimes who has been laid to rest here. It is, of course, regarded as a holy place, a waystation to the afterlife. However, there are those here who have yet to carry out any holy sacrament beyond having their newborn skin baptized. Marriage then, perhaps, though likely upon a sacrilegious acreage of golf greenery or swath of public beach sand. Or an illuminated disgrace in Las Vegas.

It puts minds and souls at peace, I suppose. Not of those lying here, but those who've placed them. One final call to the heavens that, despite the life they've led, they deserve one final chance at redemption. As if they've tried.

In the end, it does not matter. No one alive truly knows the fate of the dead. Did they journey to Heaven, or to Hell? Only the dead, eventually, will have their confirmation.

I will never forget the sound Evil made when it died in the Baxter's house one night in the fall of 1982.

The basement of the rectory of St. Ambrose had that smell. The one that appears to be common amongst cellars of houses of the Lord. Of decades-old candle wax and spent wicks, mold-imbued books. Of rotted flowers and palm reeds. That smell. I'd once thought it unique to our chosen parish at the time. It's not. And any time I happened upon it in some other basement, sometimes in another church, I'd be reminded of CCD.

Some people call it Catechism. I suppose it could have been called Sunday School, except in our town it was held on Tuesday nights. Tuesday School? Not the same ring to it, I'd say. So, CCD. Sounds like some kind of mental condition, now that I think of it. Apropos, if you don't mind me saying so.

Needless to say, I did not look forward to Tuesday nights.

The last year of CCD for me was centered around preparing for Confirmation. I won't get into the details of that for you non-Catholics, and to be quite honest I can't remember what to tell you about it anyway. I suppose it was to "confirm" one's faith in God and the church. Confirm beliefs. Confirm that you bought the whole damn thing. One of "them." One of the flock. For me it served only as confirmation that, following that fall, my Tuesday nights henceforth would carry with it only the aroma of glorious, sweet freedom. Thank you God, Hallelujah, Rama-Lama-Ding-Dong, Amen.

Father Jacobs, the presiding priest at the time, did not conduct CCD at St. Ambrose. The old guy would show up from time to time, sure, when he wasn't busy doing God-knows-what on a Tuesday evening. Probably better off pulling numbered letters out of a bingo cage, really. But for the most part it was just us ten kids and Mr. Baxter.

Of all the teachers I had for CCD throughout the years, Mr. Baxter won the prize for being, shall we say, the most devout. This includes the likes of Sister Estelle, a decrepit, miserable thing harkening from the days of when my own mother attended Catholic school in a neighboring town. No lie, Sister Estelle—or Sister Est-Hell, as we called her—carried a yard stick along her back like a rifle on a cattle rancher. I've learned since then that it served more as a bullshit deterrent than anything else. God save the poor soul warranting its unsheathing.

Thankfully, I never bore witness to it.

Warren Baxter's boys, Mark and Jason, attended this particular CCD class along with me and seven others our age. They were homeschooled, so I can't say any of us knew much about them beyond the walls of that basement and that the poor bastards had their dad as a teacher. Not just Tuesday nights, but every fucking day.

Mr. Baxter sorta reminded me of Christopher Cross. Y'know, "Sailing" and "Ride Like the Wind"? Not to mention he carried a beaten acoustic guitar with him anytime I saw him. He certainly wasn't an old guy, but he sure had what I guess you could say was an old way of thinking when it came to the education of religion. He had a habit of taking it upon himself to detour from the illustrated Jesus textbooks and remind us of all the things that could make up a mortal sin. You might think that means killing, stealing, raping—that sort of thing. No. He'd remind us weekly that masturbating was a mortal sin that was a sure ticket to Hell. Even thinking about jerking off. It was like you might as well give Satan himself a handy, because, son, it's just like knocking on his door with that hand.

I guess Mrs. Baxter was a sure help of keeping her husband Heaven-worthy, at least before their divorce.

Mr. Baxter was a parishioner at the church, but he also sang and played guitar at Sunday mass. Considering the limited source material, he wasn't half bad. I'd been taking guitar lessons at the time and knew he wasn't just some two-bit hack. He played for us a couple of nights at class, which was a welcome reprieve from mundane bible verse analysis, even if it wasn't exactly Clapton we were listening to. The man dug music, no question of that. And on the second-to-last class of the year, he took it to a new level.

The record player sat in the center of the largest table. Not an odd sight, really. We'd listened to hymns and such before, and even been forced to—dear God—sing along to them. But there was something very different about it this time. Something special. When my eyes caught it, I couldn't restrain myself.

"Zeppelin!"

Paul Morley, my best friend at the time, saw it too. *Led Zeppelin IV*, its unmistakable album cover featuring that painting of an old man lugging a bundle of sticks, sat among a few recognizable others. AC/DC's *Highway to Hell*. Queen's *The Game*. Classics today—purely defining then.

A few kids started in with "Stairway to Heaven" before Mr. Baxter shut them down.

"And she's buy-uy-ing a—"

"Sit down, everyone. Yes, I'm going to play some of these—just a little. But then I have an important story for you."

He slipped *Led Zeppelin IV* out of its sleeve and placed it onto the turntable. *Man*, I thought, *this is gonna be great.* I prepared myself for the sweet sounds of Robert Plant, belting out his "Hey hey, mama," rolling into Jimmy Page on the ax and Bonham on skins. It was already playing in my head.

Instead, we got something else entirely.

Mr. Baxter turned on the player and moved the needle up a bit onto the platter. He put it down a few times, giving us a little tease here and there of what we could have—should have—been listening to in entirety. He finally got to "Stairway to Heaven" and let it play. Sweet release.

About midway through the song, he turned the player off. *What is this, another lesson about not beating off?* I thought. To fourteen-year-old me, it may as well have been.

"Now, listen to this."

We all knew what was going to happen. Playing "Stairway" backward wasn't new. And then it all became painfully clear. Zeppelin. AC/DC. Queen? I hadn't heard about that one yet. But most of us knew of the supposed hidden messages within the latter two, and now Mr. Baxter was going to play them. Here. In the basement of a church.

He spun the record counter-clockwise, slowly, by hand. Eventually he got to the money shot, where Plant's voice seems to sing out the words "my sweet Satan," along with some other things that don't sound so Heavenly when you over-analyze the shit out of them.

But for the playing record, the room was silent. I don't think we quite knew what to make of it. Mr. Baxter—a guy who'd preached that the simple pleasures of alone time in a long, hot shower was sinful—was playing verses about the Devil. In the Lord's house! What was next, a Ouija board?

Once he was through with *Zeppelin*, he went onto *Highway to Hell*. The album cover alone should have burst into flames the moment it entered the parking lot, but he played it just the same. For a few minutes, singer Bon Scott became Scott Bon. Or maybe it's Ttocs Nob. You're supposed to hear something like "my name is Lucifer" somewhere in that backmasked garbage, but all I heard was blasphemy to some wholesome, British-born rock and roll.

Queen was an interesting one. Played backward, the lyrics "another one bites the dust" becomes "it's fun to smoke marijuana." Oh great, so now that's evil too? My older brother's days were numbered.

Mr. Baxter let the chuckles and high-fives among us slide and stopped the turntable. "All right. Why did I play these for you tonight?"

I dunno, to thank Jesus these classes are almost over, I thought.

Paula Spencer spoke up. "Because they talk about the Devil... ?"

"Not exactly."

We all looked at each other, clueless. That wasn't it? Besides Freddie Mercury soloing in reverse about weed, what else was there? And I was sure as shit stinks that Baxter had his fair share of ganja in his days. Hell, at that moment, I was thinking he'd smoked a bowl before class.

"A couple of reasons. First, it's to make you aware. The things your generation is listening to—on the radio, on records, and tapes—are deceiving you into falling out of love with God."

"But on the radio, it's not backward," Paul said.

"I don't even have a record player," said someone else.

Mr. Baxter shook his head, in that these-clueless-kids sort of way. "It's doesn't matter. You heard it for yourself. It's still there. And the Devil—he hid it there."

We learned years ago: you don't groan at a teacher in CCD. But the restraint in the room was palpable. "So... Robert Plant... is Satan?" I asked.

"No. He's just one of many instruments."

"Like a guitar?" Randal asked. Now that let loose a volley.

"All right, quiet down. Not like that, no, Randal. I mean they serve the anti-Christ. Though they may not know it. But, because we can play this... music this way, the Devil's tricks are revealed. And they are in all of the music you're listening to. All the rock and roll, all the heavy metal. It's there, and he is trying to use it to deceive you into falling out of grace with God."

"So... what are we supposed to do?" I asked.

"Stop listening to it. Forward. Backward. On the radio, or at home. These are all the new instruments of Evil. And you should shun them just as you would any other mortal sin you've learned about in this class. You'll think you have control over what you believe until it's too late, and you stop coming to mass. You stop loving Jesus and God and everything else that will bring you to everlasting life in Heaven."

Well, I was going to Hell. Before he'd finished his bummer of a diatribe, I'd started to think that if everlasting life in Satan's parlor meant a lot more Zeppelin, Rush, and everything that was candy to my ears, I might just be okay with that.

"The second reason I played these for you—and this is very, very important. You listening?"

Most of us nodded.

"Never—and I mean never—do this on your own. I know it's tempting—a fun trick to show your friends. But do *not* do it. I played this here, because we're safe in God's house. But at home, or anywhere else, you are not. And the Devil does not like when his tricks are revealed. And he will let you know."

"How?" Paul asked.

Mr. Baxter pulled out a chair, sat down, and leaned in. "I'll tell you how. Because it happened to me. Mark and Jason can tell you—they were there."

All eyes were on the two Baxter kids. Their eyes told us that either they were mortified or terrified. After what their father had to say, I'd go with the latter.

"A night a few months ago, Mark was playing one of these records in the cellar at home. I told him what I told you, many times before—none of that music. The work of the Devil. Sins against God. But he couldn't help himself. That's how it works: you let him in, and he won't let go.

"So I decided to show him what was hidden in those songs. I did the same thing I did here tonight. I stopped the record, and slowly I began to play it in reverse. And those same, hidden messages were revealed.

"And then... he walked right through the room."

"Who?" someone asked.

"The Devil," Jason whispered.

In the ensuing silence, you could hear a guitar pick drop.

Mr. Baxter nodded. "He did. A dark figure. Dressed in the darkest cloak I'd ever seen, he passed into the room. No face, just nothingness. Tears were streaming down our faces. We couldn't move. He glided closer to us, and we still could not move. He stopped just ten feet away from us, and he pointed, right at me. And in a voice I'll never, ever forget he said..."

He let the sentence hang in the air. This was some real camp-fire-story shit, and I'm betting I wasn't alone in hankering for some roast marshmallows right about then. What a showman.

"... 'No.'"

No? That was it? Not "come with me, you're going to hell" or "turn it up, man"? I say that now, but to be quite honest with you, I was shitting bricks.

I'd been taught for years every manner of how the grip of Evil might drag me down into a fiery pit of doom. You bet your ass I was saying the rosary every night and had a small shrine to Virgin Mary in the corner of my bedroom. Now I was learning that this Satan fella came in a physical form like the Grim-fucking-Reaper if you pissed him off.

I glanced over at the Baxter kids. My look said "this shit real?" Their look was "this shit real." That did it. After an extra lap around the beads before bed that night, sleeplessness would be unavoidable.

The following Sunday morning, I was once again packed hip-to-hip between my mother and brother within our usual pew at St. Ambrose. The usual congregation was there, including Mr. Baxter on guitar and frontman Father Jacobs. Paul, a four-years-running altar boy, was on the bells with Mark Baxter.

I hadn't forgotten the story Mr. Baxter told earlier that week. How could he just continue on like that, seeing what he saw? Or worse, what load of horse shit he fed to a mess of God-fearing—and now, for certain, Devil-fearing—kids? I wasn't sure what was worse: that he went so far as to convince his own boys to play along so convincingly, or that they actually did see something that night.

Paul caught up with me in the parking lot as the adults meandered around shaking hands with one another and secretly hoping they'd get home in time for football.

"What's up?"

I shrugged. I had nothing.

"Hey, I talked to Mark earlier. About what his dad said."

"What, about masturbating?"

He pushed me. Hard. I guess I deserved it. "That Devil shit."

"Paul! We're still at church!" Paul's mother hissed from somewhere in the crowd. That woman could hear a hummingbird fart in a bison stampede.

"It's the parking lot, Mom! God, relax."

If I'd talked to either of my parents the way Paul did, all the prayers in the world wouldn't protect be from the sure evil that would ensue. The Devil would walk right in and applaud. But Paul's exposure to the dictionary from Hell came from none other than his own mother's mouth, and with certain regularity. I became fluent in the language by the time I was eight, from weekly summer sleepovers at the Morley house.

"He still swears it's true."

"You make him swear to God?"

Paul laughed. "No. But he's not changing his story. Said a big person in a cloak sorta floated into the room and then back out again."

"What did he sound like?"

"I dunno. I didn't ask him. Probably like 'STOP THAT SHIT NOW!'"

His impression sounded more like Froggy from *The Little Rascals* than some dark being from the netherworld. Come to think of it, that would be pretty terrifying. Would someone please get that poor boy a cough drop, for God's sake?

"Paul!"

"Sorry, Ma! I tried it, y'know. The record thing. Nothing happened. It's a bunch of buuuuuullshit."

"Well, duh, yeah. You thought it was real? Creepy story, but no way is that gonna really happen. He was just trying to scare us. Don't you think we'd hear of it happening to someone else already? I did it at my cousin's house a few months ago."

"What happened?"

I gave him a look that told him that his stupid question was going forever unanswered.

Paul pointed to the parking lot behind me. "Look, there he is."

Mark Baxter was still clothed in his altar-boy whites, carrying his father's guitar case to their station wagon. Paul gave me a nudge and started in his direction.

"Hey. Mark."

Mark was a quiet kid, but not shy. More of a rebellious sort, I guess you could say. If he'd been in traditional school like the rest of us, no doubt he'd be one of the "cool kids" who took shit from no one and gave a pile of it to the teachers. There were few occasions you'd see him without bruises or a black eye, a sure sign he hadn't backed down from trouble. It was that attitude that made the story he was holding onto so compelling.

"What's up? Hey, Keith."

I held up a hand in greeting.

"Swear to God that story is true," Paul said. The equivalent of a religious double-dog dare. Mark shut the rear door and leaned against it.

"I'm not doing that. You know I won't do that."

"So it's a bunch of buuuuull—"

"I don't care if you won't take my word for it. It's what I saw."

"How come it never happened to Keith? He said he did it at his cousin's house, and nobody creepy came drifting through the room. Except maybe his aunt Helen. Sorry Keith, she's, like, a witch or something."

Mark shrugged. "I guess you're lucky. Maybe it's the house."

Paul seemed to back down at that. Then the wheels started to turn. "Let's do a sleepover, then," he said.

"A... sleepover? What are we, ten?"

"Well, then just have us over at night. Your dad's got the records already. We just play them in the same room, on the same record player. If the Devil doesn't show up, then it's a bunch of crap."

Mark's cool demeanor warmed at that. "My father really doesn't like people over. And it's not a bunch of crap."

"I wanna see for myself. So do you, right, Keith?"

I did my best to hide my real answer to that one. Instead, Mark did the honors. "No. You don't. And I don't, either."

"Psssh. B.S. Whatever."

Paul turned and walked away. I gave another silent wave to Mark before taking off as well.

I was only just getting ready for bed when something rapped against my bedroom window. It was early, but it was a school night, and I knew just who it was.

I opened the window to Paul's shit-eating grin. "Let's go."

"Now? Where? It's a school night, man."

"Baxter's."

"What, Mark wants us over? I thought his dad wouldn't let us."

"We're just gonna go visit. Come on."

I shut the window in his face. Paul kept right on talking.

"If you don't come out now, I'll go knock on your parents' window and tell 'em you called me over."

I flung the window back open. "No, you wouldn't. And they're not even in bed anyway."

"Fine, then I'll go knock on the door."

He wasn't bluffing. He'd done this to me before, and my folks fell for his Eddie Haskell routine every single time—hook, line, and sinker. As usual, Paul was going to get his way. I, as usual, was not.

The Baxter house was walking-distance away, but since Paul had his bike with him, I took mine as well. There's something about walking while someone rides circles around you that feels a bit degrading.

We threw our bikes onto the Baxters' lawn. I headed for the front door, but Paul started around the back.

"Where are you going?" I said.

"Mark's window."

"Jesus Christ! He doesn't know we're coming?"

"Nah. You heard him. He wasn't gonna have us over. So we'll just come over."

I really should have made for my bike and headed back home. I started to weigh the punishment I'd get from my parents due to Paul's threats against Mr. Baxter's wrath, should we knock on the wrong window. Once I got home, Paul would make good on what he said, I'd be grounded for a week—and more—and the process would repeat until he got his way. I thought it better to see it through and put an end to Paul's obsession right then.

None of the shades were drawn in the Baxters' single-story ranch, and we found Mark hanging out in one of the rooms alone with its door shut. The lights were on and he was lying in bed, sort of huddled in a ball, back to the window. He was still clothed and clearly not sleeping. I tried to convince Paul otherwise.

"He's sleeping. Let's go."

Paul ignored me and gave the window a knock.

Mark sprang up from the bed and turned to the door. "I—I'm just praying, Dad. I promise."

Paul knocked again. Mark stiffened, snapped around, and was greeted by Paul's smart-assed wave. My look said, "I know. I'm sorry. What can ya do? It's Paul."

The window unlocked and opened.

"What are you doing here?" Mark licked at a cut below his lip, and his face was sunburn-red. Always meeting trouble.

"Man. Who'd you fight this time? Did you finally fight Felix?"

"Maybe I'll fight *you* for coming here knocking on my window. What do you want?"

"Play us the records."

"Go play them yourself."

"We wanna see what you saw. Come on."

"You really don't."

"Just let us in. If you don't, I'll just go knock on the door and tell your dad you called us over." Right from the Morley playbook.

"No! Just… Fine. Meet me at the back by the bulkhead."

Mark lowered the window. Paul was already on his way to the back of the house, but I watched Mark push his bedroom door open carefully, looking around before edging himself into the hallway, and pushed the door shut without a sound.

The bulkhead was a rusty, two-door entryway set into the house's foundation. A few minutes passed before the inside latch was screeched open like a prison lock, and one of its doors creaked open. I could barely make out a person standing in the dark. I sure as Hell hoped it was Mark. Paul nudged me ahead of him. Either his night sight was better than mine and he was sure of who it was, or he just as blind and I was his shield.

"Get in," Mark whispered.

The bulkhead led into concrete-floored basement, pitch black but for a crack of faint light from beneath a closed door. The smell of mildew and machine oil was unmistakably workshop-ian. I confirmed this when I bumped into what I figured was a long workbench. A few tools clattered onto wood and clanged against the floor.

"Shhh! My dad's room is right above here."

"Where's Jason?" I asked.

"He's staying with my mom."

Mark opened the door into a finished part of the basement. All was dark but for a single lamp on an end table against a torn couch. Grey berber carpeting covered the floor from wall-to-wall, stained in the corners with water damage. French drains were always an afterthought back then, and not one easily or cheaply rectified. An old pool table took up the place of honor, consuming most of the room. Against one wall a Radio Shack–brand Realistic stereo. Of course, it had a turntable.

Mark shut the door behind us as quietly as he had his bedroom door. "We're under the living room here. We should be okay."

Paul already had the turntable cover off and was flipping through the sleeved albums stacked vertically beneath it. "Which one did you play when you saw that thing?"

Mark hurried over and pushed Paul aside. "Get out of there! My dad has them all organized. He'll kill me if we mess it up."

He pulled an album from the shelf and looked at its cover. Admiring it? Fearing it? One couldn't tell. "This one."

"In this room, right?" Paul asked.

Mark nodded.

"Where did he come from?"

Mark pointed to an opening without a door. "The laundry room."

"At my house, that's where my dad keeps his booze," I said.

"Are you sure it wasn't just your mom?" Paul said to Mark.

"What? No! My parents are divorced, stupid."

"So maybe it *was* your mom."

Mark said nothing, but the seething in his posture was palpable. At that moment, I felt sorry for both of them.

Mark eased the platter out from the sleeve and placed it on the turntable, then turned the receiver on. He grabbed the needle and halted before placing it down.

"I don't think you want me to play this backward. It ruins the record, anyway."

"No, we want you to play disco so we can dance," Paul said. "Just play it. I want to see the Devil you said you saw."

I finally spoke up. "But what if—"

"But what if what?" Paul snapped. "We see him and he tells us 'no' again? So what? Then we know and we won't do it again."

Mark looked back at us both, then placed the needle down. He seemed to know just where it had to go. "This can play the record backward on its own. I don't need to do it by hand."

He flipped a lever on the turntable and stepped far away, eyes not leaving that laundry room door. At first, seconds of silence, but for the popping and crackle of worn vinyl, then the speakers came to life. Sure enough, the words of Robert Plant from Led Zeppelin's "Stairway to Heaven" began to blast in reverse. I was caught off-guard at how loud it was, on account of Mark's fear of alerting his father to the goings on.

It caught Mark by surprise as well. "Shit!"

He stumbled to the stereo. Someone appeared in the doorway to the dark laundry room. Mark froze. We all did. Satan had come. And then he spoke.

"What did I tell you?"

We said nothing. I felt the urge to run, but my legs were no better than bowling balls on Twizzler sticks. Paul backed up and was stopped short by the pool table. The record kept on playing.

"What. Did. I. *Tell. You!*"

Mark spoke. "N-No?"

"No! Nobody over! *Nobody!*"

Mr. Baxter stepped into the room. He was seething. He was nothing like I'd seen him before. And he was clearly loaded.

"And are you... are you playing that again?! After what happened last time?!"

"Dad? I... I'm sorry. They just showed up. I didn't know—"

"Shut up! You two, get out of here the way you came!"

Through this all, the record continued to play, but all I could hear was Mr. Baxter's rage.

"And you! Get over here!"

Paul and I turned tail and blasted through the door into the workshop. Paul shut the door behind him. "Holy shit! His dad is... He's crazy! Let's get the hell outta here!"

For once I was willing to following Paul's lead. As the bulkhead lock slid open, I heard Mr. Baxter's anger turn up to eleven, while Robert Plant carried on.

"How many lessons do I need to teach you, Mark?! Another one?! And another?! I guess it's time for one more! Come here!"

Mark started to cry. "No, Dad. Please."

I couldn't move. I knew that plea all too well. To leave, or stand idly by, knowing what was sure to come next, would be as damaging as what that bastard was about to do.

"What are you doing? Let's go!" Paul said and then flew out into the yard.

I turned and opened the basement door. Mr. Baxter had Mark pinned against the wall by the stereo, his arm cocked back with a fist. The record skipped. I'd say it was comically timed to my entrance, but the situation was anything but.

I've carried on a lot about how strange Mr. Baxter was. How he seemed to thrive on using the fear of damnation as a demented teaching tool, to kids who had been taught throughout their lives that Hell was no place to wind up. Throughout lessons failing in everything but illustrating the absurdity of it all, he had been kind. He had been patient and good. A seemingly willing volunteer to God. In that moment, the fog had lifted. Like with the ridiculous things he preached, he had fully veiled the truth of himself.

Mr. Baxter's head snapped in my direction. "I thought I told you to—"

My mouth opened, but nothing came out. My breath caught in my chest. My eyes were no longer looking at Mr. Baxter or Mark. The anger that had been blazing within them turned to absolute terror, trained on the open laundry room door.

The being floated into the room.

Mr. Baxter dropped his arm and flattened himself against the wall next to his son as the record played on.

Tattered dark brown robes draped over what was mostly human-shaped, drifting about it within a nonexistent wind. Swirls of debris and filth floated within the gaps of the cloth. Though they could have been flies, as the sounds of Led Zeppelin seemed drowned out by a skittering, hissing sound that bordered on radio static. There was no face, no real body parts at all. Just a thing. I would say it stood about seven feet tall, but that wouldn't be quite accurate. Because the best I could tell, it was floating.

The thing drifted closer to the Baxters. Mark continued to cry. Mr. Baxter looked as though he might start. Neither one said a word.

A long piece of the thing's robe lifted, as though carried by an arm that wasn't there, pointing, at the abusive wretch against the wall. It spoke.

"NO."

Mr. Baxter broke down and slid to the floor. His mouth moved the words of the Lord's Prayer, though I couldn't hear him over the hissing, the music, and the throbbing in my head.

Mark didn't follow suit. Instead, he ran over and stood beside me.

"NO," it hissed again.

"Please."

"NO."

"No. I know. I know," Mr. Baxter whimpered. "I'm sorry. I'm sorry. I know you said no. I won't do it again. I won't do it again. I won't!"

"COME."

The specs floating within the swirl of robes darted to where Mr. Baxter lay huddled on the floor. There was no music, only the sound of what had begun to consume Mark's father within a cloud of black, black that became solid, almost gelatinous and liquid. He screamed as the mass took over the man's shape, writhing on the floor in what appeared to be pure agony.

The screams became grotesque, muffled gurgles before ceasing as abruptly as the thing had appeared in the laundry room doorway.

Mark turned his face away. I still couldn't move at all.

I have no idea how much time had passed before what had overcome Mr. Baxter once again became a cloud of airborne debris. On the floor, another stain to match those in the corners of the room, this filling the room with the odor of stale urine. As though called back to their master, the specs drifted to where the robed thing hovered, wafting about it as they'd done before.

It didn't go back into the laundry room. Instead, it was just gone. Just as was the music. Just as was Warren Baxter.

Outside, I wasn't at all surprised to see Paul and his bike long gone. I'd been inside with Mark for a long while after what had happened. He was a raw mess, as anyone would be. I helped him give a call to his mother, who lived about an hour away. I stayed for about that long before walking my bike home—I was in no condition to ride.

"I'll say he just left me here," Mark said. "Nobody would believe me if I told them what really happened."

"What about his car?"

"He walks a lot. Usually to the bar down the street. They'll believe that. I know Mom will."

I could tell you I was terrified, walking that stretch of road alone late at night, after what I'd seen. In truth, I was relieved. For so long I was told of mortal sins I thought frivolous as being the true path to Hell. That simple "impure thoughts" would destine me to a horrible eternity only a young, teenage boy could imagine. How could such things measure in defiance of all that is good to the monstrous acts of murder, or of rape, or of beating one's own child? There was a comfort in knowing that once the Devil truly is in someone, he comes looking for that piece of him to take home.

My house was in complete darkness. I threw my bicycle into the garage and entered through the back door, into the kitchen. At that hour, I was sure everyone was asleep.

"Where've you been?" It was my father. The son of a bitch was standing in the doorway from the basement, in the dark. Ice cubes tinkled from his highball glass.

"I... was just putting my bike away."

"No. You were out. All night."

"Dad, I—"

"Get in your room."

There was no point in carrying on. I did as he said and shut the door behind me.

It was a school night, but I wasn't about ready to sleep. Sleep, I knew, wouldn't come at all. Not after the Baxter's. Not after Dad. It would be another day of looking tired, looking terrible. All under the guise of looking tough.

"What are you doing?" I heard my mother ask from down the hall. "What time is it?"

"Your son. I'm getting my belt."

"Adam, no..."

I turned on the small stereo in my room. *Led Zeppelin IV* was already mounted on the turntable, affectionately played countless times in the past as I fought to sleep through a shroud of tears and pain.

I placed the needle down, and as the door to my room opened, I began to turn it counter-clockwise by hand.

THE HAMMER'S NAIL

*D*o you know the history of Saint Ambrose? I do not mean the history of the saint himself, but here. The church. The cemetery and mausoleum. No, I suppose you do not. There aren't many who do.

Name aside, Ambrose was originally built in the Highlands of Scotland, many centuries ago. It was known by another name at that time, one that I cannot recall. It was eventually laid to ruin by townsfolk in the region for being, shall we say, unaligned with their ways of things.

The stone of that very church was brought here. It was a rather large monastery, you see, so a good portion of it makes up the Saint Ambrose church, as well as the main mausoleum. Why they could not make use of materials of the region, I cannot say.

Builders have peculiar superstitions of how things are made, I suppose, especially when concerning places such as this. Most especially they are particular of materials with which they are built. The chisel's stone. The shovel's earth. The axe's tree. And, of course, the hammer's nail.

"Careful, lad," Kinnon's uncle Edan warned. The boy was all of ten years but built more like thirteen. His sweaty face shone from the glowing embers of the forge, and his stringy black hair dripped and hung over his brow. "You do not want to drive the bellows too hard now. Our coal stores remain low until Mirren returns."

Kinnon stopped pulling the bellows' rope and caught his breath a moment before speaking. "When does Mirren return, Uncle?" he asked.

"Not until the next thaw, I'm afraid."

Edan stopped his work at the anvil and snatched his water bucket's ladle. It overflowed as he pulled it to his face, a nest of a course, red, ash-coated beard that hung to mid-chest. He spent no time caring whether the ladle's contents entered his mouth or rained down upon the rest of him. Cleaner water would have come from south of the town, at the River Forth, though the smithy's work at hand and his tired bones meant the soot-filthy bucket water suited well enough. Presently, the room began to darken from the lack of air-fueled fires.

"Do not let up just yet, lad! Just bring her down easy. We do not want the forge cold now. Keep her just right."

Kinnon put his weight back into the rope, though this time less forcefully. The heavy counterweight raised, the bellows took in breath, then exhaled into the forge's flames with the rope's release. The room was once again filled with an orange light, arid heat, and the acrid smell of exhausted coal. In times past, the boy's limbs would have trembled from the arduous and repetitive work, but he was five years at the forge now, and he'd become well accustomed to spending countless hours fanning fires. The young apprentice had patiently awaited the day his uncle would pull him from the bellows to the anvil, where he might finally set hands on a black-smith's tools.

"An armorer needs first to understand the fires, lad," his uncle had said one evening, over a meal of stewed venison and potatoes. "Then he learns of the ores and of their smelting. Only then will he be ready to begin forging."

"But I do not want to be an armorer, Uncle. I want to make great swords and battle axes, and weapons for the three-feathers!"

Edan took a long draw of mead from his flagon, not removing his eyes from the young boy. "Let me ask you this, lad," he said. "What will these great weapons of yours be used for? What might their purpose be?"

"Why, to win battles and wars, of course," Kinnon said, without a moment of hesitation.

Edan eased his flagon onto the table, then slammed his fist down hard. The sudden action caused Kinnon to jump. "That is only the purpose of the one who wields it, nephew!" Edan exclaimed with irritation, his finger pointing stiffly at the young boy as he spoke. "Swords are not what you will be making in my forge. My anvil has not touched the side of a blade since before your father set off. I do not intend for it to see another!"

"No weapons?" Kinnon snapped with disbelief. "Did you not once forge great claymores in your fires, Uncle? Why no longer? The other children say—"

"Your uncle has said his peace, Kinnon," the boy's aunt Kyla interrupted. "It makes no matter what others are saying."

Up until then she'd sat listening to the two squabble without adding a word, sipping careful spoonfuls of stew from her bowl. This, however, was not a topic she cared to see carried on, though she spoke with more kindness than her husband. "Finish your stew, then off to your chores, lad."

Kinnon let the topic die, but his uncle's words did not deter his wants. Forging polished steel plates of armor to be worn in battle was a great thing, to be certain, but songs were not sung of the great deeds a breastplate made in defeating enemies.

Presently, the setting sun cast a faint glow through the small windows of the forge, their thick panes of glass long since filthied and rippled from years of the nearby forge fires. Edan's hammering rang out quieter now, quick and deliberate, as the finishing touches were made to give the piece its final form. As another hour passed, he at last set his hammer down and turned the cooled metal over several times, inspecting his own handiwork. Kinnon continued at the bellows, if for nothing more now than to keep the room from descending into darkness and cold.

"Your tenth year," Edan said, without taking his eyes off the unpolished greave he'd last been stamping into shape.

"Uncle?" The boy let go of the bellows' rope and picked a bright coal from the forge with tongs. Using the hot ember he set two candles alight on the blacksmith's workbench, then tossed the coal back to sputter out with the others.

"This winter is your tenth year, lad. I mark every one of them, there." The blacksmith pointed to a support timber beside the room's only door. Upon it were horizontal notches carved deep into the wood, of which there were nine. The boy wasn't sure why he hadn't noticed them before.

"Nine winters," Edan said. "This now marks ten." His voice was sullen now, and he cast his eyes downward at the formed piece of steel that suddenly felt very heavy in his hands. He fell onto his stool and let his arms drop to his lap.

"What is it, Uncle?"

Edan lifted his head and swept his gaze across the room, looking through his nephew as though he wasn't there and as though he was seeing his forge as it had been over a decade ago.

"You heard true, lad."

"Heard true of what, Uncle?"

"I was once a maker of weapons. Great weapons, for the clan chiefs, and the chieftains, and for many of those they led."

Kinnon's eyes lit up then. He snatched another wooden stool and planted himself onto it, within an arm's reach of his uncle. "I knew it was true! What kinds of weapons were they, Uncle?"

"Many kinds, lad. Maces. Daggers—beautiful blades, aye. Axes of all sizes. Swords, of course. War hammers..." At those trailing last words, Edan's eyes met Kinnon's. The man's gaze was filled with pity and regret.

"But why no more, Uncle? These are great things you once made. The high ones surely still carry them by their sides and across their backs!"

"Still carry them, they do, aye," Edan said. "And there are others who carry them as well."

"Others?"

The blacksmith leaned forward, staring at one of the lit candles across the room. Its light flickered as cooler outside air crept through unseen cracks in the room's walls, its vague pillar shape sitting upon a growing flat puddle of melted wax. He sighed heavily, realizing the moment he'd known would one day come was upon him then. "It is time I told you of your father, Kinnon."

At that, Kinnon's excitement faded in an instant, replaced with a mounting dread. He knew his father had succumbed to an untimely fate, though what that was he had never been told.

"Your brother," the boy said nervously. "Connell Gowan."

"Connell. Aye, Connell was his name. But my kin by blood, he was not."

Kinnon sat upright in his chair, taken aback by his uncle's words. "Not a Gowan, Uncle? I do not understand."

"I made a promise to myself and to my dear Kyla that, in your tenth year, I would lay onto you the truth."

"But why are we speaking of him now, Uncle? Was my father one of the others you made weapons for?"

"Aye, I did make a weapon for Connell once, though he is not one of the others I speak of."

Kinnon kept silent, then. It was not the time now for more questions, and he let the air sit heavy and quiet while he awaited what more his uncle had to say. Why had a conversation of weapon forging turned to talk of his father?

"Connell was of the Buchanans, from the isles to the west. He traveled to our town by way of Stirling, some nine summers ago. A quiet one, he was, though that was made up for by you, the weeping wean he carried. Just the two of you; he came with little else. Some thought he might be one from the feuding clans, or perhaps a fugitive or deserter. A kidnapper. There was no denying you were his, that much was certain. Shared the same eyes, you did. And there was no mistaking the love he had for ye. Why someone would come upon our small town, though—from Stirling, no less—no one knew. But come, he did, seeking a bed, and work to pay for it. Of that, Kyla and I had both, so we took ye both in.

"Your aunt and I had no children of our own. We tried, truth be told. God... had other intentions for us. Connell was a fitting father, to be sure, but Kyla and I felt just as much parents to you as though you were our own. Your mother—"

Edan cut himself off, for a moment not realizing to whom he'd been talking. This, he knew, was not the portion of the story he'd been dreading to tell, and softening the telling of it would do no good.

"Connell said to us that your mother died after birthing you. That was all we knew. Not long after, Connell had left the isles with only you and what little else he could carry. We did not know why he left. Perhaps it was grief, we thought. It made no matter. I was happy to have his help in the forge, and we were both happy to have you.

"Connell, your father, had your same locks—coarse, black as night, to his shoulders—though none upon his chin. He was a bear of a man, I tell ye. A quiet giant, he was. Your father was a natural smith's striker. Tireless with a sledge. What took any smith worth a crown three days to shape took Connell but one. This he did for us, and we paid with meals and a square of straw to sleep upon. He asked for nothing more, and he would have taken nothing more that we would offer, if we had not insisted.

"Truth be told, we did not have much more to give the lad," Edan continued. "Kyla has a skill with wool, to be sure. She crafted blankets and clothing for the coming winter for ye both. These things we could give you, though they are but objects of need and survival, not symbols of gratitude. He loved us just the same for it, Connell did. Connell loved, and he was loved. It did not take long."

Edan took several long pulls on his beard, as he often did when feeling troubled. The boy continued to sit in silence, ever attentive.

"There came a time when word arrived, from clansmen across Stirlingshire, of the need for arms. Your father and I were called to task, and day and night the forge rang and roared. Its fires never ran cold. Mirren of the mines could scarcely supply us with coal and ore with enough haste. Those we made the weapons for grew impatient at our pace, but alas, we were two men with the task of ten. Our finished work was that of twenty skilled men, and of that all of Stirlingshire had not. So, with us, the restless remained restless, and in time their sheaths embraced newly forged and sharpened steel made by our hands, and we would not see of them again.

"Connell was a quiet man. But I told ye that already. He did not speak much about his past, and I did not care to bother him with the telling of it. I know well enough when a man has chosen to keep a tale only to himself, and no amount of taunting or gold or tankards of mead are enough to loosen their tongue. I know, too, the price of hearing their once-sealed words. They cannot be unsaid or unheard, as much as one or both may wish them to be."

Edan closed his eyes and fell silent then, contemplating the very words he'd just spoken to the boy. Were these words best left unsaid and unheard? Would the boy who had become like a son to him become a better man in knowing?

"Aye," Edan said to himself. "This, you must know."

"Uncle?"

Edan looked up then and met his nephew's expectant stare. "The warring clansmen came no longer, and the forge had become cold and still. We had no further need for Mirren, and we were glad for the respite. Aye, all of us were. Upon the first snow, I was at last able to bestow upon your father what I had been making without his knowing, past nightfall whilst the calm had come and the house slept on. A great claymore, one of my finest blades of steel, to be sure. Its edge could nay have been sharper, its blade no more polished. Kyla made for it a fine grip of beast hide, finished with a pommel of ivory, carved with the rampant lion of Buchanan. Connell was not one to take gifts, as I told ye, but this he accepted with no ado. Your father had worked in the forge enough by that time to know what such a blade meant. It was not a thing to be turned away.

"The snow's image casting back from the blade matched its pommel with a blinding white. Connell took to naming it the Ivory Nail. Hah! Such a massive nail! 'Twas a good thing, to hear that your father could jest."

Edan paused for a long moment, turning the greave over several times between his hands. When he spoke again, his tone became one of resolve.

"Clansmen passing through oft brought down tales from the fields of battle, both great and small, though we knew many of them to be tall. Some told of a monstrous beast of a man, of Clan MacLaren, who had been sending many of their brothers to graves. Cast a shadow twice the length of any commoner, he did, clad in full iron plate and helm, blackened and twisted as though it had been chewed by the mouth of Hell and spit out upon him.

"The Ebon Lion, he was called. It was here I sat on this same stool, and your father on yours, when through that door he came. Afore him was Kyla, with you wrapped in wool and tight to her breast. He pushed her forth and to her knees. Connell and I came to our feet, and it was then we saw the tales were true.

"Connell, as I said, was a lofty one, but The Lion stood well-nigh an ell taller. The crest of his helm passed far above the crossbeams, and the top of his faulds met me at the neck. Wide as a barn door and near half as thick, he was. Armor black as coal, misshapen by the fierce punishment of untold foes.

"The open door brought in the cries of women, children, men, animals; the smoke of homes and granaries put to torch. Our town under siege. Our defenses broken. The towering monster struck the door closed and threw his helmet aside to the floor. The longest sheets of hair, he had. Poured beyond his shoulders, slick with sweat and black as night. Over his face, it hung, and all but his grotesque mouth could you see, half-filled with corrupt teeth. His breath came foul and heavy, a cloud of grey from the heated cold, much as when a hot iron is put to water, and it reeked of death.

"He said nothing and put his hand upon the handle of the great hammer strung across his back. I thought for certain he meant to do us all in right then. Instead, it dropped beside his helmet. A fierce war hammer it had once been, afore the spike end of its head had broken and become worn to nigh flat. Its iron handle had become as bent as a longbow. The blunt of its head was carved as that of a lion. Such work I had not seen outside of my own forge. Covered in dried blood, it was, head through stem. He need not have spoken to know why he had come."

"Mend the hammer?" Kinnon murmured.

Edan nodded. "Alas, with the pillaging carrying on beyond these walls, to restore such a thing would take more time than The Lion had patience. Still, he sensed my hesitation, drew my Kyla up from the floor by her hair, and with his other gauntleted hand he grasped her throat. His hand came around her neck as fully as a common man's might grasp a child's arm. Kyla let out a hideous shriek, and it took all I had and more not to come at him then. It was his voice that stopped me cold. No man I have heard before or since had one such as his. Thunderous and loaded with rage. It reeked of hatred and corruption and an evil what only holy men had been told of by God. He said but one word: 'No.'

"I was left to choose, then: repair the monster's deliverer of death, so that he would continue to paint it with the blood of my clan, or refuse and watch as Kyla's precious head fell to the floor from his tightened grip. It made little matter. The Ebon Lion would see that we few within this forge would see no further days than that, no matter my choice.

"There was another sound, then. Above clamor and chaos, there was heard not a wail but the softest of cries from Kyla's arms. 'Twas you, lad, waking as from a dream, not knowing of the nightmare at hand. The Ebon Lion heard you as well. His other colossal hand reached to that bundle Kyla held. It was then that the choice was made clear, and it was one your father made, not I.

"Connell, our beloved quiet giant. He was quiet no longer, for within that man a fury such as fire flew forth, fiercer than that which boiled within the blood of battle-hungry men.

"'For my Moira!' he cried, whilst he rose and brought his Ivory Nail down upon The Lion with both hands. Sword passed through iron, flesh and bone as easily as a hot blade would part ripened cheese. The arm was severed at the wrist, and it crashed like a felled tree limb beside the hammer and helm. Though great torrents of blood so dark as to be black poured from where an arm once was, the Lion made no sound. Nary a grunt."

"That monster... killed my mother," Kinnon said in realization within the ensuing silence. "Moira was her name? And my father—he slew The Ebon Lion for her?"

"Aye, Moira, she was. As for what you ask of your father, you know there is more yet to tell of him, lad, or else he would be the one here doing the telling."

Kinnon nodded solemnly and turned his eyes downward.

"Having but one hand did not slow that beast," Edan continued. "Now he threw Kyla down, again to the floor, though still her arms held you. On her knees, she came to my side as quickly as her legs would allow. Nay, though, could I take my eyes from your father as he pulled at his sword. So strong was his downswing that it had become driven deep within the floor. I... moved quickly to assist him, but my breath was taken from me, for I was thrown far onto my back before my foot fell forward. The Lion had struck me, crushed the bones within my chest with the backside of his full arm.

"I saw... I saw him draw up the mangled war hammer. Blood shone wet upon it, though now from the pool left by his fallen limb."

Edan pointed to the floor behind Kinnon, where a dark stain fell like a permanent shadow upon it. The boy turned to look, remembering what he'd always know was there though never once asking about, along with the two larger ones by the door.

"He brought the hammer above him. I could see his eyes, then, through his matted mess of hair. Pale and lifeless, they were, without color or pupil, as those of blind men. His mouth 'twas a gaping abyss of anger, so truly twisted and foul. I had no doubt in me, then, what was to become of us. Aye, this new fury in him had become unbridled, to be set upon us all.

"But he turned away, to Connell. And then... then there was The Nail. Through the back of the Ebon Lion, a hand's length of sharpened steel came. It was with a strength beyond that of any one man that Connell had freed the blade from the floor, drove it fully through the beast the moment he faced him. So much blood there was.

"The floor became thick with it, and the air turned rank. Connell withdrew the claymore, though the beast kept his feet, still with his hammer high. Before The Lion's next drop of blood touched the floor, Connell's Nail came around in a blur and parted The Lion's head from his neck. It fell hard upon the floor and rolled beside the fallen helm, as though the two were in some way drawn to one another."

Kinnon jumped from his stool. "Hurrah! He did! Killed the Ebon Lion! He protected you and he protected Aunt Kyla! And me! A hero, he was!" The boy swiped at the air with an invisible sword, as if dueling an unseen foe. "And what then, Uncle? What happened to my father, after he brought the beast down?"

Edan let the boy enjoy his swordplay a moment longer before he spoke again. "Kinnon. Sit down, lad."

Kinnon let his arms drop to his sides and slowly took to his stool once more. The blacksmith looked very tired, then. He swallowed hard, then reached out with a slow and heavy hand, placing it upon the boy's shoulder. "Kinnon, dear boy. Your father was a hero; you have the truth about that. He protected me and Kyla... and you. Alas, he could not protect himself. There is no other way to tell ye the rest than with all the grim truth of it. The Lion found strength to bring the great and bloodied hammer down, in spite of what Connell had done. It was the Ebon Lion's final act... but with it he had made Connell's in saving us."

The two turned their eyes toward the floor, to the spot of which, until that moment, only Edan had known the source. The emotions that ran within each of them, unique: Kinnon, that of pride and wonder; Edan of sorrow and regret. Edan stood and walked slowly to the cooling forge, its embers still hot though casting a barely discernible glow about the room. Once again he started to pull at his beard.

"You say a weapon's purpose is that of winning wars," Edan said, his back turned to the boy. "Many weapons help win great wars when put into the hands of those set to win them. It is the purpose of those men to win battles... or lose them. Aye, great battles are lost, Kinnon. Battles both great and slight. They are lost by the just, and they are lost by the unjust.

"What does it mean when it is said to win a war? Mayhap one counts those with the least fallen? The side not to have fled in retreat? Is this the outcome a sword seeks? Its purpose?

"A hammer may help the builder make a stable, but 'tis only the nail the hammer seeks. A pickaxe does not look to raise great castle walls for kings; it merely begs for a stone to part. A sword—a weapon—strives not to win wars, Kinnon; it seeks but to smother the fire of life."

Edan turned around to face Kinnon, who sat upon his stool, taking in every word from his uncle.

"I said I had not seen a hammer the likes of the Ebon Lion's outside of this forge. 'Tis because here 'twas made. I am not certain how The Lion came upon it, but have it he did, and with it he dealt more death... more death than I care to wonder."

The blacksmith exhaled deeply, a sense of both exhaustion and relief washing over him. As one not known for having the need to keep secrets, he'd just released a great one, and the freeing of it gave him a great sense of calming and liberation.

He'd grown tired of tugging at his whiskers in front of the boy he'd taken in as his nephew and son. It was time, he knew, for this boy to have known the truth and to become a man.

"That is all I have left, lad. All that's left to tell, and all I have left in me for it. You know now of your father, your mother, and the fall of the Ebon Lion. And mayhap you know now why my forge will ne'er alight again for the making of a weapon. As a sword seeks to kill, armor seeks but to protect. Aye, many of my swords remain in the hands of those in battle, and though I provided them to men on the side of the righteous, I know some will fall, and into the scabbards of the sinful they may be. Leastways my armor will see to it that weapons will find it much more difficult to take what they seek, sinful or not. I'll have no further part in filling crypts with the dead."

Silently, Edan and Kinnon left the forge, out into the dark winter, for their home nearby, where no doubt Kyla had prepared another evening's meal. Kinnon not once inquired about the Ivory Nail, nor did the subject of forging weapons leave his lips again.

He knew, too, what Edan and Kyla had done for him at his father's passing.

Unconditionally, they loved him. Like parents, they nurtured him. As armor upon one whom swords may seek, they protected him, with wise words as much as a warm hearth.

Upon the arrival of Mirren and the thawing snows, Kinnon MacGowan—the only kin of an armorer of the Highlands—entered his uncle and father's forge once more of many times to come, this time with ten notches upon the wood by the door. He took to the anvil as Edan tended to the coal, and the springtime air rang with the sound of steel upon steel, as a new breastplate slowly took form.

SCARS

As you can rightly tell, the hands and minds of many have taken part in the forming of these great halls and grounds. It has taken numerous forms and transformations throughout the years.

The first crypt, for instance. I am told it seems to have been lost to time, dormant and forgotten, somewhere beyond what has become the bordering forest line. I haven't bothered myself to explore for it. Truth be told, I am privy to quite enough to know not to.

I often think of those who had sacrificed their time and bodies to our cause, to clear trees and overgrowth, to lay the foundation and walls of a now disregarded resting place, once again reclaimed by the Earth. Ironic that a tomb for the dead should become, itself, entombed.

Were those builders alive today, what would remain as evidence of their toil? Rumors, perhaps. Stories told by an old sexton? One can always choose not to believe the tales they are told. Doubt, though, would slip away, once gazing upon the hands and bodies of the laborers, evidence of their deeds drawn upon them in scars.

I don't go into the woods. There are things in there, things that drive my anxiety through the roof at the mere thought of coming close to them. A casual hiker may not notice them, lying low and deep within the surrounding foliage. On a windless day they remain perfectly still. They don't have to make a move. You'll come close soon enough, and then they're all over you. You won't know of their effect until you're tucked away in your tent. Or in your bed at home. The next day—oh boy, the next day. Then! Then you will know. And then it's too late.

But I see them. I can't not see them, because they are fucking everywhere. When walking down the street. At the playground. Even in my goddamn back yard. Jesus, my palms are itchy just thinking about them.

They have become the most frightening living things to me in my little corner of world. I cannot believe that God had chosen to create these things, for poison ivy, poison oak, and poison sumac are clearly the work of the devil himself.

My brother grew up allergic to peanuts. For my sister, it was cashews and pistachios. This was the deadly kind of allergic, where not the slightest whiff of these nuts could pass by their nostrils without cause to whip out the epinephrine shot. Unlike my siblings, I was lucky enough not to have food allergies of any kind. However, growing up in a household without peanut butter in days before alternatives like almond butter were commonplace meant I had no concept of a good ol' PB&J. Jam and butter? Not even close.

Though I was clear of food allergies, there was something I did have to stay very far away from: poison ivy. Poison oak. Poison sumac. The poison plant trifecta, I call them.

This was not your run-of-the-mill allergy, mind you. While 85 percent of the population is allergic to these plants, most would need to come in physical contact with the leaves to have some sort of reaction. This was not the case for me. A slight breeze off a plant several feet away would carry enough urushiol oil through the air to latch itself onto me. Then came the warm redness later that night. Sometime the next day came the itching. My god, the itching. All from walking too close to the side of the road on a windy day.

One of the worst episodes I'd experienced came when I was a boy, while helping my father stack a cord of apple wood he'd cut down that summer. Apple wood, as I was told back then, is prime stuff to stoke the stove with in winter. I suppose it must have a sweet, burning applesauce smell to it, but what do I know? And what did I care? I was getting paid ten dollars! This was going toward the gaming console I'd been dreaming of for months: the Atari 2600.

Under a blistering sun my brother and I hauled split wood onto the bed of my old man's truck, working well past sunset. Sweaty and sunburned, we left not knowing of the full conditions we'd been working in. The logs had covered the immense patches of glistening poison oak that'd I'd otherwise have steered well clear of, had we seen them in the light of day.

The next morning, I could not open my eyes. My face was swollen to the point of being unrecognizable. My hands were bloated sausages, covered in liquid-filled skin bubbles. My inflamed feet wouldn't fit in my shoes. My hearing was partially affected because they'd been so engorged with blisters. It even got inside my nose and on my scalp.

I must have gone through fifty bottles of Calamine lotion that summer, that awful smelling pink shit you coat on your rash in hopes of relief from the incessant itching. It would do the trick for about an hour if I was lucky, and then I'd be painting more of it on, again and again. I looked like the Elephant Man covered in concealer.

I'd resorted to drastic measures at times to alleviate the swelling. I would take a sewing needle, for instance, dip it in rubbing alcohol, then lance the pustules between my fingers in order to drain them enough that I could bend my fingers to hold onto a fork or even wipe my own ass. And yes, the poison oak got there too. But that's not the worst spot to get the itch.

The soles of your feet, the palms of your hands. Nothing is worse than that. Not even your balls. Calamine lotion doesn't work on soles and palms, and the itch is unending and unbearable. Placing my palms on something hot, however—say, a leather seat that'd been sitting in the sun all day—somehow provided some brief reprieve. The searing pain was much more tolerable than the itching; in comparison, it was ecstasy.

Overall, not a good summer. But I did get my Atari.

Now, Ted. Ted was a different story.

There were a few times I'd gotten bad cases of the poison ivy plague during the school year. Maybe not so bad as that summer of blisters, but once bad enough that I was kept out of sixth grade for several days. My absence did not go unnoticed by Ted.

"You were out for three days because of... poison ivy?" he said, the two of us standing at the edge of the schoolyard during recess. "Just because you got a rash?"

"Just a rash? Haven't you ever had bad poison ivy before?"

Ted shook his head. "Don't think I ever got it at all."

My jaw fell. "Never? Not even a little?"

"Nope."

"Well, count yourself lucky. It sucks." As I said this, Ted wore that faraway look of his that I'd seen too often. The kind that says there's an idea brewing within that thick skull that's boiling into action before it's had a healthy seasoning of reason. A true recipe for disaster that I'd seen all too often.

"What's it look like?" he asked, his eyes scanning the ground amongst the dense thicket of brush nearby.

It didn't take me long to point them out. I'd been eyeing them since we got there, and I'd known they were there since the school year had started. And I presently stood as close as I was ever willing to get. I pointed to the glistening patch of leaves beneath a crop of trees.

"There's a bunch of it right there," I said. "Those green leaves with red. A ton of it."

Ted didn't hesitate. He was halfway there before I could raise a stink.

"These right here?" he called out. His pointing finger was so damned close to the poisonous bouquet. My mind's eye saw the slick oils drifting through the air and onto his willing, exposed skin, and I shivered at the thought of being remotely as close to it as Ted was.

I nodded. "I'd get away from it if I were you."

Except he wasn't me. The ridiculous idea of his had already bloomed in his mind and he was dead set on seeing it through. He stepped directly into the patch. He picked one of the leaves. Then another. Then a whole branch. I couldn't breathe. My own skin began to feel hot at the mere thought of being in Ted's shoes, shoes that might not fit his feet anymore.

My god, his hands, I thought. *His fingers. His palms! Dear lord, his palms!*

It was like watching someone bite into the hottest pepper in the world with idiotic, wild abandon. But this was worse. Much worse. The mouth-burn of a Carolina Reaper may feel like the fires of a thousand suns, but that's an agony that's short-lived. Ted was in for days of hell on Earth.

"Wh-what are you doing?" I breathed. It was then that I noticed I'd been subconsciously distancing myself from the whole scene, as though Ted's disturbance of the plants would affect me where I stood. In fact, even at ten feet away—for me—that wasn't far from possibility.

"We got that math test tomorrow," he said. "With Ms. Sullivan?"

"Yeah, but—"

"Well, I'm not going to be here to take it." He took the words right out of my mouth.

Ted bunched the leaves in his hand, as though what he held were harmless bits of greenery and not the evil carriers of Hell oil they were. I knew it was too late for him then. Unless he immediately scrubbed his hands with rubbing alcohol, he was in for it. And I, for one, was going nowhere near him at that point. Best friend be damned; as far as I was concerned, he was a walking plague.

But he didn't stop there.

I didn't protest. I couldn't protest. And if I could have, it wouldn't have mattered. At best, my words would have been unintelligible gasps and stammers. Anything worth hearing would've been ignored. All of his chips were pushed to center now; he was all-in.

As one might clean themselves with a bar of soap, Ted began to rub the poison ivy all over his body. Arms. Legs. Face. For good measure, he replenished his supply of leaves when he'd rubbed some down to bits of pulp, then did the entire exercise again. Just when I thought he was through, he did the unthinkable.

He turned from the rest of the schoolyard as though he were about to sneak a piss, pulled the front of his jeans out with his empty hand, and jammed the other hand in. And then his hand came out empty.

It was suicide. I was witnessing my best friend's self-immolation and couldn't move a finger to stop him, for in doing so I'd surely be dooming myself.

"Think that'll be enough to get me out of school tomorrow?" he asked.

"What did you do? That's enough to keep you out for, like, a month!"

He pumped his fist. "Yes! Even better!"

My eyes didn't leave Ted for the rest of the day. Where he sat. What he touched. What urinal he used. Short of wearing gloves and a mask, I behaved like some crazed germaphobe. And as far as I could tell, Ted wore that bunch of leaves down his pants all damned day. Pants that I hoped he'd set fire to come the next day, along with the rest of his clothes, once he realized the enormous mistake he'd made.

Side note about fire and poison ivy. Fire, as it turns out, is not an affective eliminator of urushiol oil. I learned this the hard way, of course, during my junior year of high school, along with a sizable portion of my fellow classmates. One of the rare times I dared enter the woods was for high school parties. It was isolated, difficult for the cops to get to, and had an unlimited selection of places to hide in and make out. When no parent-free houses were available, it served its purpose well enough.

Besides an abundance of cheap alcoholic beverages, a natural ingredient of a party in the woods is a bonfire. And a natural ingredient of a bonfire is wood. Or, at least, a combustible material of any kind. Sometimes a tire; sometimes the back seat ripped out of someone's shit box. And sometimes random brush. In this case, on this particular evening, brush entangled with poison oak. And a byproduct of a bonfire? Smoke, and lots of it. It gets in your lungs, your hair, your clothes. And you bring that all home with you. If you're not completely shitfaced before attempting to crawl into bed, maybe you take a shower, therefore not waking up the next afternoon smelling like a campfire. And, if you were somehow thorough enough, perhaps you don't succumb to the full onset of the poison oak you'd been hanging around in all night.

Like me, everyone—save for a few—spent at least the following few days in hell. From that point, not only would I stay far from the woods, but I'd also go nowhere near open fire pits save for ones fueled by gas. Until then, I'd never known what it was like to get poison oak in your mouth. Or on your dick—everyone's got to take a leak at a raging beer party at some point.

And here Ted was about to get the full experience, his first time.

When I finally saw Ted exit the school bus that afternoon, I was sure it was the last I'd be seeing him for a good long time. I wouldn't be paying him a visit any time soon, that was certain. Except I didn't have to.

The next day, Ted walked onto the morning bus like nothing had happened. In fact, nothing had happened. Ted, as it turned out, was among that meager 15 percent of lucky sons of bitches on the planet who's not affected by urushiol oil at all. No blisters. No rash. Not the slightest itch. And while I was pretty sure he'd taken a shower that morning, I still kept my distance from Ted for that day and the next. I did not want to take the chance. And though Ted felt he was in Hell for having to take Ms. Sullivan's math test that day—a math test he clearly had no intention of preparing for the night before—in my eyes, he surely did not understand the massive bullet he'd dodged.

Some have said that it's possible to outgrow an allergy to poisonous plants. There are others, still, who claim that actually eating one can trigger an immunity. After thirty-some-odd years of systematically weaving and dodging my way around any suspect crops of leaves—whether consciously or not—I never had the intention of finding out, most especially not by making a goddamn salad out of it. I'd grown accustomed to avoiding the shit. My quality of life hadn't suffered at all because I didn't go for deep-woods hikes or take up camping or trail jogging. The memory of my childhood suffering had scarred me for life; I was not keen on ever revisiting it, and certainly not on purpose.

Ted and I kept very close for a long time. Our wives hung out together. Our kids went to the same school. We attended the same church. We even started a business together, a pizza and sub shop—Giuseppe's—that somehow resisted being muscled out by booming franchises. Ted was the real talent behind the place, having developed most of the recipes himself. His pizza sauce was unmatched, which largely accounted for the loyal customer base. I was the business side of things because, if you haven't caught on, Ted was no good with numbers; he couldn't count out proper change for a dollar. And I was lucky if I could make a cheese sandwich.

We were called upon to cater the annual Saint Ambrose church picnic. This was last summer, with days hotter than the deepest ring of Hades, and the comet making its lasting streak across a bit of the night sky. Pot luck alone was insufficient for the large gathering, and so Giuseppe's filled in. On the house, of course. It was our parish, after all.

Naturally, both of our families were there as well. My wife and son, Ella and Peter. Ted's wife, Kim, and his daughter, Sophie. Truth be told, it was as boring an affair as always. The adults got by with chit-chat and gossip. The kids had to get creative to remain entertained: ball, Frisbee, hide-and-seek—that sort of thing.

Saint Ambrose owned a large, empty parcel of land adjacent to the church. Most of it had been cleared years ago to make way for an expansion of the cemetery, the old one having been filled to capacity, the old mausoleum nearly there as well. No vacancy, I guess you could say. The dead check in but they don't check out. Nothing unnatural about it, really. Just old people getting older and drunk people getting dumber, for the most part. It's so old that some early Scottish immigrants had their names chiseled on stone there; it was bound to fill up at some point.

Sometime just before noon, Sophie came running over to us from the clearing. She wasn't in tears, but she was not happy.

"Daddy! Peter lost the Frisbee on us, and now it's not fair because he said he won't help me find it!"

I hung my head, exasperated. I cupped my hands to my mouth and called out. "Peter!"

Ted clapped a hand on my back. "Hey. Don't get too mad at the kid. It's just a Frisbee."

I shook my head. "It's the last Giuseppe's opening-day Frisbee I have. Remember those? With the corny phrase you put on it? Besides, that's not the point. And I can only take his ten-year-old attitude so much, y'know?"

"Oh no, I wouldn't know anything about *that*!" Ted laughed. "Let's go find your kid and this damned Frisbee. And, hey, that phrase isn't corny. It's poetry!"

I had a laugh at that as we dropped what we were doing and headed in the direction Sophie had come. As we crested the small hill, I caught sight of Peter in the distance, standing just outside the edge of the woods. His back was to us as he stared into the trees beyond.

"PETER!"

"Hey, hey, hey," Ted said with a gentle tone of reassurance. "He's right there. Take the anger down a notch."

I wasn't angry. In fact, so far, my son was doing just what I hoped he'd do. Just what I'd taught him to do. Or, rather, not do.

If you don't know exactly what's ahead of you in the woods, you do not enter.

And when did anyone ever know exactly what was in the woods, even ten feet in front of them? That's right: not ever. Could be ticks or snakes or a covered-up hole atop a vast underground chasm. Or, need I say it, poison ivy.

Peter turned his head to us at the sound of my voice. His expression was of concern, though from fear of getting in trouble or of what he'd been looking at, I couldn't say.

"What's up, kiddo?" Ted said. "Go on in and get the Frisbee. It's not gonna bite ya."

"I'm pretty sure that's not what he's afraid of," I said. Ted looked to me with a bit of a puzzled expression. I returned it with a raised eyebrow; he knew what I was getting at.

Ted shook his head and sighed. "Oh, for crying out loud. Where is it, Pete?"

Without turning back around, my son pointed directly into the woods.

"In there. *Way* in there. I can't even see it, but I can see tons of—"

"Tons of poison ivy," Ted interrupted. "Right. Right. Your dad's got you all worked up about it because he blows up all like a balloon near it. Am I right?"

"Come on, Ted," I groaned.

"Kinda," said Peter. "Only the stuff in there is, like, a lot bigger. And there's something else in there too."

"Yeah, the Frisbee!" Sophie called out.

Peter ignored her remark. "There's a... tomb or something in there. Next to the huge leaves. Dad... it..."

Ted chuckled, though his tone was touched with concern. "A tomb, Pete?" he said. "What are we, in Egypt?" Ted sometimes had a fine way of making it difficult to discern the adult from the child in his conversations.

"I dunno what you call it," Peter said. "It's, like, one of those things in graveyards with a big door on it. Dad, there's sounds coming from inside it. Like, voices."

"What, like a crypt?" said Ted. "What the heck is one of them doing in the woods? They ain't started putting graves out here yet. Look at it. It's been one big, open field for years. Must be something else. Don't let some pile of logs or whatever scare ya. Think the ol' Crypt Keeper's calling you to come visit? Probably left over from when they started clearing it."

Sudden realization seemed to strike Peter then, in why he was standing with us, explaining himself. And so he began to ramble on in one breathless plea.

"Don't let them make me go in there, Dad. That thing scares me, and then there's those huge shiny leaves, and you told me to stay away from those and never touch them so I shouldn't go in there! And there's voices in there! Really! *Please!*"

"Okay, okay. Take it easy," I said. "No one's going in there."

"Hell with that," said Ted. "I'm goin' in. Poison ivy never got me before. Won't get me now. And the Crypt Keeper's a little shit."

"And you," Ted continued, pointing an accusatory finger at my son. "You should take more responsibility next time. If getting a little itch is what it'll take for you to do the right thing, then so be it."

Before I could argue with Ted's attempt at re-parenting Peter, he approached the edge of the forest and parted a mass of low-hanging pine branches, then stopped.

"Ho-ly…"

"See!" Peter said. "You see the tomb in there, right?"

Ted took a moment to answer as he appeared to survey what he was looking at.

"Yeah," he said uncertainly. "It's no pile of logs. Looks like an old crypt, all right. Pretty old one by the looks of it." He turned to look at us. "This was an old cemetery before?"

I shrugged. "Not that I've ever heard."

"I mean, there's no headstones, no other graves. Just… that. In there."

"Well, that's not creepy at all," I said. "Just leave it, Ted. Seriously."

"Damn. Kiddo's right about the leaves too. Like the size of elephant ears."

"Oh, come on," I said in disbelief. "Then those can't be—"

"What did you say?" Ted interrupted.

"I was saying that those can't be poison ivy. They aren't that large."

"No, no," Ted said, holding up a hand behind him. "It wasn't you. Shh! You hear that?"

"Hear what?" Besides the distant commotion from the party we'd left behind, there was nothing. I looked at the kids who were both slowly backing away, shaking their heads in the negative.

"Ah! There!" Ted shouted, now uninterested in whatever noises he'd been hearing. "There you are, you blue bastard. Frisbee's right there."

He parted the branches further apart and stepped deeper into the woods, disappearing from sight. The sound of breaking branches followed as he marched inward, spattered with moments of colorful cursing. After about ten seconds, there was nothing.

"Daddy?" called Sophie. "Did you get it?"

A few seconds more. Nothing.

"Hey Ted!" I called out. I silently prayed that I wasn't going to have to enter those woods to look for my friend, but the crack in my voice said it all.

Branches cracking again. Ted was running for the clearing. He burst through the overhanging branches where he'd entered, panting, red-faced, and sweating profusely, no Frisbee in sight.

"Daddy! Where's the Frisbee?"

Ted was doubled over, hands on his knees, catching his breath. Sweat soaked his shirt. His face. His hair. Even his shorts. Ted's not exactly in shape, but he's not morbidly obese either. A ten-second run in dark woods shouldn't have exerted him like a marathon.

"No Frisbee, sweetie," Ted said between wheezing gasps for air. "Like your uncle said, we'll buy a new one."

She began to protest. "But it—"

"Sophie, no. Just... go play with something else. We're gonna go home soon anyway."

She crossed her arms and stormed off.

"Uncle Teddy," Peter said. "What happened in there? Did you hear the noises from the tomb?"

Ted stood upright and gave me a look that said he wasn't up to talking to a kid about this.

"Pete, go catch up with Sophie," I said. "We'll probably be leaving soon too."

Peter did as I asked and disappeared over the hill.

"All right, so what did happen in there? You look like you just came out of a rainforest."

"Man, that is the spookiest damn thing I've ever seen."

"What, the crypt?"

"Well, yeah, the crypt, but not just that. The kid wasn't kidding about the sounds from it. Like... I don't know. Voices. And, damn, those leaves. All over the thing. They... You wouldn't believe me."

"All right, you've succeeded in freaking me out. They what? Talked to you?"

"Moved. Not from wind or anything like that. I marched in the middle of them to get the damn Frisbee, and then something just felt... off. Like I thought maybe you'd come in behind me, only I knew you'd never do that, but it felt like someone was there. But it was just all of those plants, all around me.

"And then they moved. Not from the wind or anything like that. It was like they were turning to... I dunno... to look at me.

"Well, I turned and got right the fuck outta there and left that damn Frisbee for those fucking plants to play with."

I snorted, and then the chuckle just followed it on out. I couldn't help it if I tried.

"Oh, okay," Ted said, my laughter becoming too contagious for him to avoid. "I see. So why don't you go on in there and get the thing? Damn zombie plants from the crypt. You'll see!"

"You know, I'd clap you on the back, but you're sweatier than a Ridley Scott movie."

"Ha ha. Well, this ain't sweat. It's dew from all those leaves in there."

I stayed far away from Ted for the rest of the walk back. I told myself as much as Ted did that the leaves were just covered in dew. How could all that be urushiol oil? It just couldn't be. But the scars upon the memory of my youth endured, and so I took no chances, even at the expense of Ted's playful jeers.

Soon after, each of our families ended the day and went our separate ways.

Ted didn't show up at the shop the next day.

Ted would usually open the place up in the morning in order to get it ready for the lunchtime crowd. I'll stroll in sometime later, before we actually open for business. Only this time the doors were locked. Ted hadn't shown up yet.

I unlocked the place and went inside to call Ted. After a few rings, Kim answered the phone. She sounded like I'd just woken her up.

"Hey, John."

"Morning. Sorry, did I wake you?"

"No, I just... didn't get much sleep last night. Exhausted."

"Is Ted there? He didn't show up to the shop today. Place was still buttoned up when I showed up."

She sighed with exhaustion and frustration. "Oh god. I'm sorry, Ted. I should have called you. Ted's worse off than me. It was his tossing and turning all night that kept me up. I eventually had to sleep on the couch. Looks like he... caught something at the picnic yesterday."

"What, like a stomach bug?"

"No, no. Looks like he got too much sun. Worst sunburn I've ever seen, the poor guy. But I guess it serves him right for not putting on sunscreen. You know how pale he is."

"Paler than a beluga whale, yeah," I said, punctuated with a sigh of defeat. "All right, so I guess he's out of commission today. Tell him to call me when he's up and about."

She acknowledged and hung up. I went about making a closed sign for the door and directing our phone to a voicemail message stating the same. There was no way I was attempting to run the place without Ted.

I left and spent the day doing long-neglected chores around the house. Spending time with Ella that day made me realize that we'd both somehow come out of the previous day with nary a scant tan, much less evidence of a sunburn. What's more, it was an overcast day—we hadn't worn any lotion.

Later that night, my cellphone rang. It was Ted. He sounded as ragged as Kim had that morning. "Hey, man. Sorry I didn't call you sooner."

"Yeah, sure," I said. "Don't sweat it. You all right?"

"No. No, I'm not."

"Jesus. From a sunburn? How bad can it be?"

"Sunburn? No, this ain't no sunburn. Gotta be poison ivy. Itches like fucking hell."

It took all I had to keep the phone in my hand as my mouth fell open. I suddenly felt my own skin begin to take on that characteristic burn. My palms begin to itch, my mind telling my body that it, too, was once again stricken with the rash. The mere mention of it was enough, like an instinctive cringe. What's more, Ted of all people had succumbed to it. How?

"But I thought you weren't allergic," I managed to say with some measure of disbelief.

"Yeah, well. Shit happens, I guess," he said. "Listen, I gotta go. It's... God, the itching is... I have to go."

Before I could ask about what we should do about the shop, he hung up.

It's not unheard of for someone who'd once had an immunity to something like poison ivy to suddenly lose it over time. Ted suddenly showing signs of a reaction normally wouldn't have surprised me. In fact, his lack of a reaction in all this time was the more surprising thing to me. And more surprising than all of that was how quickly it had taken hold on him. He'd gone from zero to one hundred seemingly overnight.

There was nothing I could really do for Ted. He'd seen first-hand what I'd gone through in the past, what meager remedies I'd resorted to for alleviating the itching and swelling. It's all I could do then and all he had now.

I faced the fact that it was clear Giuseppe's was staying closed for at least another day. Depending on how bad off Ted was Tuesday night, I'd have to consider my options, like hiring some temporary help. I wasn't the best cook, but I could at least keep the business afloat.

Late the next morning, I gave Ted a call to see how he was faring. He'd likely faced another sleepless night, so I wasn't surprised when Kim picked up.

"Hey, Kim. How's Teddy doing? Hope you at least got some sleep last night."

"I slept okay. Ted didn't sleep in the bed all night, stayed closed up in the den all yesterday and last night. Didn't want anyone to go near him. Trust me, we didn't want to. He was in a mood, as you can imagine. I woke up a couple of times in the night and heard him downstairs, grunting, swearing. It must've been driving him nuts.

"But... I guess he must be doing better. I woke up to the smell of him cooking breakfast, not that he left us any. Just a dirty skillet. Nice, right? And now he's gone off somewhere."

"Seriously? He went out?" Though I was amazed Ted hadn't gotten worse overnight, I was relieved.

"Maybe check the shop?" Kim suggested. She'd read my mind.

When I pulled up to Giuseppe's, I noticed one of the exhaust vents on the roof billowing smoke. More than usual, in fact. Ted's car was nowhere in sight, which wasn't entirely unusual, since he lived only a couple of miles away and sometimes made the walk. I thought this a good sign, that Ted really was on the mend and getting things prepared for the afternoon customers. Except when I got to the front door, my "temporarily closed" sign still hung in the window. I figured Ted hadn't noticed it, so I pulled it down as I entered.

I could hear Ted busy at work in the back kitchen. The air was already hot with the warming pizza ovens, griddles, and fryers. One of the oven doors had been left opened, and I could see the remnants of what looked like a pizza mishap smeared upon the oven's firebrick floor. Pretty early for pizza, I thought, but we served all kinds.

"Ted! You back there? What happened here? Oven's a mess!"

The sound of the kitchen fryer answered, its contents being lowered into the 325-degree oil. And then something else: a man's exhale of intense relief. No, it was pleasure.

I rounded the corner into the kitchen. Ted's back was to me, facing the fryers. He wore nothing but a pair of boxers, and his skin was like nothing I'd seen before. My sneakers squeaked to a halt as my breath caught in my throat. I stumbled backward, catching myself on a counter. Oozing sores covered half Ted's back and legs. The other half was covered in blisters the size of golf balls.

"Ted," I managed to breathe as I fought back hyperventilation.

Of course he couldn't react. Because when I say he was facing the fryers, I mean that in a much more literal sense. His entire face was submerged in the steaming fryer oil, up to the hairline. I would've thought him dead, but a second later he stood upright. Grease poured down over his shoulders and trickled down his back. More of the blisters withered and broke apart under the oil's heat. And once again Ted sighed in ecstasy.

"Ted!" What was meant to be a scream came more like a strained whisper. I threw a hand over my mouth, either due to pure disbelief over what I was seeing, or to stop myself from being sick, or both.

He straightened and turned around, my feet instinctively making a slow retreat sideways, toward the door. What I was looking at was not Ted. Not anymore. This person was unrecognizable as a human being in all but frame.

Strips of red, smoking flesh peeled away from his forehead and cheeks, the bare muscle and bone behind glistening with oil. Lips…

there were no lips. A set of teeth in a perpetual, skeletal grin, the tongue behind, bloated and red, peeking out behind them. Eyelids hung like useless flaps. His arms, his chest, all bare of skin, looking like an anatomy poster. His arms, blackened and charred. All that seemed to remain intact was most of the surface of his legs, and I could see blisters there continue to form before my eyes.

"John," Ted said, his voice guttural and nearly unrecognizable, but calm and eerily satisfied. "John, you were so right. Fuck the Calamine lotion. Fuck all that shit. All you need to do to get rid of the GOD DAMNED itching is HEAT. Once you've got that... oooh... it's euphoria, Johnny. Pure. Fucking. Euphoria."

He held up his hands, then. Hands that I hesitate to describe beyond that they were surely not usable appendages anymore. Something fell from what used to be his face onto the floor, joining a mess of fried flesh within puddles of spent grease.

I couldn't touch him. Jesus. I couldn't stop him. "Ted. Oh, Ted. No, no, no, no."

He breathed a wet sigh again, somehow peeling away a flap of loose, cooked skin from his forehead with one of his red, bony fingers. He threw it aside like a rotten slice of tomato.

"It's okay, John," he gurgled. "It's almost all gone now. Just a little more heat, and I'll be all better. This is so much better than the oven."

He turned back around and held his breath, as I held mine. I turned and ran.

When I made it outside, I called 9-1-1. The police and ambulance arrived moments later. I watched as EMT after EMT entered and promptly exited, retching into the flower beds outside, before finally composing themselves to enter and save Ted's life. I was told if they'd been only a few minutes later, he'd have been gone.

In all my life, I'd never seen a reaction to plants like that, let alone experienced it myself. What further floored me was that this had been Ted's reaction to whatever was in those woods, a man who'd been immune to poison ivy for as long as I could remember. What would those things do to someone like me?

I talked to my wife and told her she'd have to pick Peter up from choir practice at the church that afternoon. I also called Kim, and she and I spent most of the day at the hospital. Not a stitch of him was not covered in thick bandages, and he lost most of his fingers. The CDC was apparently being called in, and we were told Ted was going to be put into an induced coma. I couldn't bring myself to see him like that anymore, and I wasn't sure what to tell Kim about what I saw at the shop. How was I to explain to anyone that he'd done this on purpose?

An accident. A pure, unfortunate, unholy accident. That was enough.

I wasn't sure if Ted was going to pull through. There was no doubt that his recovery, if he had one, would be agonizing. At the cost of removing whatever pure hell he'd been experiencing before, would he say it was worth it? I couldn't fathom. Covered in pure scar tissue and skin grafts for the rest of his life, it's unlikely he'd have to worry about something like poison ivy ever again.

My mind, just as Ted's unfortunate body, would be scarred for life.

I called for a car to take me home. I was in no condition at all to drive.

As I exited the car at the bottom of the hill, I heard Peter call out from the driveway. "Hey, Dad! Catch!"

I was still dazed from what had happened earlier and had little time to react. Stars blossomed in darkness as whatever Peter had thrown smacked me in the forehead and fell to the ground, and I along with it. I put my hand to my throbbing head, pulling back to see blood.

"Damn. Well, that's gonna leave a scar," I muttered to myself.

Peter ran up and squatted beside me, his face reddened with embarrassment. "Oh, man! Dad! You okay? I'm so sorry! I thought you'd catch it."

"Yeah, well, my reaction's not all it used to be."

I reached down beside me to pick up what Peter had thrown. Ted's poetic words upon a plastic platter of blue greeted my disbelieving eyes.

DOUBLEBREAK

Fly In To Giuseppe's Empty. Fly Out Full.

A LAMENT FOR THE DYING

A service for the dead is a celebration of the departed's life, so we here proclaim. And so it should be, would you not say? Certainly not of their death. Of course, there are unsavory types who are celebrated more for their leaving than of their living, though these markings are rather personal and fleeting, and certainly have no place to be carried out at Saint Ambrose in the present day.

Alas, it is often not until their death that the deserving of respect gains their commemoration. Perhaps it is their intent to be recognized more in a past tense than a present. Or perhaps they would rather not be remembered at all, for the thought of true finality is foreign and daunting. To those unfortunate enough to see and fear the inevitable conclusion approaching, I offer you condolences and, with sincerity, a lament for the dying.

I like it when I die. Except today. Today, dying sucks. "This is a good day to die." Low Dog first said that, at Little Big Horn. It wasn't

Crazy Horse like most people think, and definitely not Klingons. But today is not a good day for that. It's a pretty awful day for that, if you want me to be perfectly honest. And why shouldn't I be? Honest, I mean. It's the last thing anyone's going to get out of me. Might as well cut the bullshit.

You want to know which was my favorite time dying? The first. Nothing's beat the first time. Not in all these years. Sounds weird, I know. All this time—all these deaths—and there wasn't a time one topped the first? Nope. It's like your first girl. A first child. Skis on virgin snow. Nothing like it.

Battleship explosion far off the coast of San Diego. Twenty-seven other men died with me that day. The lot of us were on the upper deck when the blast went off. Sent every one of us clear to kingdom come. I remember the feeling, being airborne like that. The roar and the heat of the flames at my back. The salty air lightly stinging my face, with the blueness of the ocean coming to meet me. I think back at that moment often these days and wonder: what if that time—that very first time—had been the last? The satisfying final act in what's now become an overextended performance. Like a TV program that doesn't know to quit on a high note, a series finale that should be orgasmically fulfilling but only flounders and flops. On and on it goes. Just when you think it couldn't get any better, you turn out to be right. But the greedy bastards running the show don't hear that. They hear syndication dollars. "Seriously? That's it? After all that, this is how the whole thing ends?" And then we shrug it off and move on to the next thing. And the next. A final footnote in Wikipedia, and that's that. Sometimes the end pans out, but most times it's disappointing. Like now.

Who would've thought I'd go out like this? Like this! Majaris. She knew. She was the one who was responsible for starting all of what I am, did you know that? Kicked the whole thing off. Back then, that... that gypsy—fortune teller or whatever she was telling people she was—said to me that the signs told her I'd be living a long life of defying death. But, "Gordy," she says to me. "Gordy, in the end, death will defy you." Death will defy you. Damn right.

I would've settled for other ways to go. Like the bar fight in Arizona. Ah, bar fights. I seemed to find myself in the middle of those the most. Sometimes I come out of them with just a few scratches. Arizona, though... that was a proper end. Full-blown gun fight. Took one point-blank and between the eyes from a piece of shit they called a Remington '75. I flew back and clear through a window, landed so hard I broke my leg along with the porch boards. And did I laugh my ass off. When I found out it would take over a year to recover from that, I wasn't laughing so much anymore.

But I kept myself busy and out of trouble. For the most part. Was back doing what I do in only three months. Will wonders never cease?

I've been banged up plenty of times before and since then, though not nearly as bad. There are the bar fights, of course. Had this freak in full armor crack my shoulder with a nasty-looking morningstar. Had a Louisville Slugger swung across the back of my knees once. Still hurts to think about that one. Even been pistol-whipped by a German Luger. No permanent injuries, but I sure got my bell rung time and again.

I've had my share of close calls too. This one time, out on the rock, one of my so-called colleagues was supposed to drive a shiv though my prison uniform while I leaned against this barred door, you know, make it look real convincing and all that. Moved more than a hair too far to the left and nearly nicked a kidney. I got transferred to a local hospital for a week to heal up from that one.

See, that's the big misconception people have about me. I can be broken, get sick. I get hurt. I get hurt a lot. Sometimes it sticks, and sometimes, well, I breeze on through it. I patch up, heal up, hold my chin up. And then I move on, just like I always do. Or I guess I did.

I always knew when I was going to die. I don't mean now, I mean all the other times. You know, when it wasn't real. This... this damn near snuck up on me. And now here it is. It's real and it's bearing down on me, and I'm pissed off. That's why I'm passing what little time I have left to talk about the good old days. So many years. So much younger. And, God damn it, so much fun to die.

Remember that time my head was cut clean off my neck with a chainsaw? Oh, that's right. Way before your time. But holy hot damn, what a messy scene that was. The only lasting damage was how long it took to get my fucking hair clean! God as my witness, my tub ran red for three days after that. Smelled like holy hell. Like the time with the guts. You know, from when the Vietnamese landmine blew the lower half of my body off. Right, right—way before your time. But I've told you this before. Anyway, guts were spread out all over on the ground. Even I thought it was for real that time. I had to wait a good two hours before it was clear for me to get back up again.

You know, like I said, I knew what I was getting into. Even then, I knew what was coming.

Gah! Why did I wait so long to drink this? Who says the older the scotch, the better, eh? I've traveled around with this bottle of rot-gut for God knows how long. Or how far. Now here we are, finally with a fitting occasion for cracking the damn thing open, and it might as well be cat piss. Bleh. I'll have you know, I was never one for the hard stuff. At least not this old Scottish shit. Fucking Scots. Can't tell you how much trouble they've caused me.

But wine. Wine has always been my poison préféré. But it doesn't keep as long as people think, either, if you want to know the truth.

It's good that I can talk to someone who knows what I can do. I haven't really told many people about, you know, what I am. Thankfully it doesn't really come up very much. I sometimes get older people who think they've seen me somewhere before. I just laugh and brush it off, tell them they're senile and change the subject. I've got no family to speak of. Not anymore. Who's left?

No one. Just me. But they all knew. They knew what I was. And you know what? All that fear about me made them care all the more. So why in God's name am I still hiding from it now? I tell ya, I have no idea.

I've been to countless shrinks, you know? I told them the real deal, and they all listened. They played their game, told me I had a gift and all that and that I shouldn't have to hide it from people. Right. Susan found out the truth, when we were dating. Thought I was nuts. Then she left me. So what the hell good did all those head shrinkers do? They made it worse is what they did. Made me crawl further down into my hole.

You know what the most ridiculous thing about all this is? Anyone who doesn't know about me can figure it out easily enough. Easy-peasy. Dig around with a computer. Find an old photo here and new photo there. Put two and two together, you know? It would only be a matter of time.

But I'm through hiding. It may be a shitty thing to die like this, but I am going to die—right here—and the bullshit's tagging along. At least I have that going for me. So bring it on, death! I may not be ready to take your ugly ass on this time, but I am not afraid! I will finally plant my ass into that empty seat at the Devil's table, look that bastard square between the horns and say, "Well, you got me, you foul son of a bitch! Now pass me that bottle of piss-swill you call wine and toast to me—that's right, to me—the late Gordon Wheeler! A cheater of death and a master of lies! For he has come here hoping that this shit hole called Hell is ready for him, for he is far from ready to retire." Won't that be something. Maybe I should look forward to that moment. Maybe it's not such a bad day to die after all.

<u>IN MEMORIAM Gordon D. Wheeler 1928—2015</u>

Gordon Dennis Wheeler was born August 28, 1928, in Chicago, Illinois, to Roy and Martha Wheeler, and passed away June 28, 2015, in Los Angeles, California, after suffering a long illness. He was 86.

Having spent most of his early childhood in several Illinois suburbs, Gordon found early work as a performer with Madame Majaris's Circus Maximus, initially as a stunt clown and later advancing to become a main performance for the event, for a brief period. During his time at Maximus, he was discovered by famed filmmaker and director Aaron Ruston, who went on to employ Gordon as a stuntman in many of his most well-known films.

Gordon's first Hollywood appearance, the 1946 action war film *The Battle of Two Bays*, went on to win several Academy Awards, including Best Special Effects.

Gordon eventually moved to Los Angeles, where he continued to perform death-defying stunts in seventeen of Ruston's films, including westerns *Henry's Apostles*, *A Native in Bisbee*, and *The Roar and the Thunder*. Other appearances in non-Ruston pictures include the Vietnam War epic *The Eight of Clubs*, and the premiere of the slasher flick series *Blood of My Blood*. At times, Gordon served as a stand-in for rehearsal performances, including several scenes opposite actress Susan Franks in the film *Sovereign's Daughters*.

Gordon has no surviving family. He was preceded in death by his brother, Raymond, and his nephews, Donald and Jacob.

A celebration of Gordon Dennis Wheeler's life will be held on the grounds of the Saint Ambrose Mortuary and Funeral Home on June 30.

EMPTY

Do not tell my employers or our clients I say this, but I will admit it is a strange place, this mortuary. We store here what souls have departed, and for what purpose for the deceased? They are but empty shells, left to decompose until one day they are but piles of fine dust. Should they not be laid to rest in the earth, to be reclaimed? Carried upon the wind as ash? Seems a selfish waste to the planet we live upon, locking them away within everlasting stone.

For the loved ones of the departed, it is understandable that it gives them peace to know that, within these walls, behind engraved signs on marble doors, there is still something physical that remains. Merely relocated, a new home. And so they visit, bring flowers to unseeing eyes and and unsmelling nose; speak to unlistening ears. To them, it does not matter that though there exist many forms of decomposing flesh here, they are devoid of their purpose—their being, their souls—and are now and forever empty.

Like water through a sieve, the sand streams through cracks between the fingers of my cupped hands. Piles form where they fall, tiny mountains of pink on an otherwise mostly flat landscape. There are much larger piles, too, far off toward the northern shore. And there are other things, not formed by the natural passing of time and trade winds, but by a force I still can't comprehend.

And then there's Scott.

We awoke on this pink blotch upon the ocean nine days ago. Neither of us recalled the events leading to our marooning here. As if the world had blinked and forgotten our place. In one moment our feet were caressed by waves of a rising tide as we sat in lounge chairs on the crowded, public beach—blink—and here we are. Quiet. Empty. Alone.

Marooned.

Exploring our new surroundings didn't take long. What I suppose is an island seems rather small, covered in a powdery, pink sand unlike that of the beach we'd suddenly left behind. An impassable, mountainous wall lies a hundred meters or so from the shore, a small stream of fresh water flowing from a crack and into the sea.

Far atop the rocks lies a solitary palm tree. We'd been in New Hampshire a moment before—the palm tree was as out of place as we were.

If not for the stream, the unrelenting sun would have surely caused our demise within a day.

We saw no signs of life beyond the two of us and the single tree. No sea life as far out as we could swim. No overhead planes. No distant ships. No crabs shifting through the sand. Nothing to satiate the hunger that was quickly setting in.

Three days into our isolation, Scott woke me before the morning sun took hold.

"There's someone here!" He seemed delirious.

"Someone else? Where?"

He was already running off to the far end of the beach. I'm not sure how he had the strength; I was barely able to get to my feet, let alone maintain footing in the unnaturally soft sand.

I caught up to him a few minutes later, breathless, unsteady, and unable to comprehend the scene. Beside where Scott knelt was an intricate sand sculpture of a monkey, laying there as though sleeping.

"Look at this," Scott said. "No way this is natural. It's too perfect. Someone made this. Recently."

I wasted no time in asking the hows and whys about it. "Hello!" I called out. "Is anybody here?! Hello!"

I stumbled the beach for hours, calling out until hoarse. The only reply was the gentle lapping of ocean waves and my own echoes off the distant wall of stone.

Scott broke his foot the next day, attempting to climb the steep incline of rock.

"I'm so fucking hungry," he said through gritted teeth. "I thought I could get a coconut, leaves, anything from that stupid tree up there. Shit!"

"I'm starving too," I said. "I guess you can eat me if I die before you do."

"No fucking way!" he protested. "I'd eat this sand before I'd eat your flabby ass."

At that we both laughed, the first time since we'd washed up here.

The next day were the crabs. I found them some ways from where the monkey had been, which had by that time become a mere pink pile. Crabs made from sand, seven of them, perfectly crafted, no detail expended. No footprints or other traces of their creator remained. I attempted to call out once more, but my voice croaked and drowned in the wind.

I trudged further up the beach and came upon a large mound of sand that seemed misplaced. Something stood out at the pile's edge: a worn, sapphire-studded, silver crucifix. It was the first real sign of the civilized world I'd seen in days besides the bizarre sand sculptures. I'm not a holy man, but I slipped it onto my neck, a sign of hope that we really weren't as lost as we thought, that rescue was inevitable before real starvation took its toll.

"Tomorrow it'll be a week," Scott mumbled in the dark. The glowing hands of his watch showed just past eleven, its date six days from our first here. "I have to eat something, man. I'm not sure I can take this much longer."

He was right. He was much leaner than I. For once my weight was working in my favor.

I woke to the sound of Scott eating something. My first thought was that he'd finally snapped and decided to eat his own, limp foot. Instead, I found him doing just what he'd promised.

"What are you doing?" I asked. He turned to me, face powdered in pink.

I watched in disbelief as he threw handfuls of sand into his mouth, licking his lips between each helping. I reached out to stop him, but he swatted my hand away as though I were trying to steal.

"Get away from me!" he growled, sounding muffled and inhuman. "Get your own! There's a whole beach of it!"

I limped away and leaned up against the rocks, the shadow of the lone palm extending ahead and toward the water's edge. I let sleep once again take me. I was so goddamned hungry. Too tired to think, too tired to save my friend from eating himself to death. I almost envied that he'd found a way out, and to be happy about it.

I woke at 12:17 a.m. to check on my friend. The time glowed off the hands of Scott's watch when I found him, the sculpture of him curled fetal where he'd last been, the pink granules of his content face sparkling in the starlight.

The last granules of sand empty from my hands. I dig in for more and eye the large mound of it that was once my lone companion in this godforsaken place. With wind and time the pile will flatten, and all that will remain will be the watch, an empty, makeshift tombstone.

As will be, once again, this silver crucifix.

HIT HARD

What brings one to be in a mortuary, I ask you? And to that you may rightly say, "Why, death, of course," hm? Death, yes, for those who are laid here to rest. But then you are thinking just as a young sexton would—brass tacks and all of that—not as a seasoned one such as myself.

To "be" here does not merely pertain to those we tend to, nor to us caretakers for that matter. There are those who are ever-present in Saint Ambrose yet are physically many miles away. Their minds—their hearts, you see—seem never to be free to leave. We cannot see them, but I dare say they can be felt.

Death of a loved one can have such effects on those left behind. There are those who choose to willingly go where their minds tend to take residence, here within these walls. Yet others choose to try to forget and let their thoughts wander homeless and alone. For them, the pain of acceptance is too great to endure; they are not yet ready to face reality.

When reality becomes realized, I'm afraid it will not apply with a soft and gentle touch. Resistance will all but assure that the truth will hit hard.

He's talking again. Why is he talking? Jesus Christ. And my tie. Feels so goddamn tight. Like I'm being choked to death. Maybe if I just stick my finger in there, pull it out more. Get some fucking relief. But I already did that. God damn it, why can't I fucking breathe?

"Bucky."

What the fuck does he want now?

"Buck! Were you even listening to me just then?"

"Huh? Well, yeah, I—"

"Bucky... This is what I'm talking about. It's what we talked about last week. The last time we were sitting here."

"Uh huh." Maybe if I unbutton my shirt a little at the top. God, it smells like... I don't know. What is that? Old glue or something? God, it's, like, burning my throat. How the hell does he stand it?

He's standing up now.

"Look, I know you've been through a lot, but for crying out loud, it's been six months."

Six months.

"It's not just that you don't have your head in the game anymore. It's the lying. I mean, you're doing it all the time now. There's only so much I can take. I shouldn't have to take any of it, really. And I can't. I can't cover up for you anymore."

He's still talking. How can he stand sitting in this box all day? Shit, would he just open a fucking window, for God's sake? He must be some kind of absurd vampire.

"I've done all I can, all right? You've gotta believe that. Chapman's on everyone's ass this quarter. We either hit it hard or get hitting the pavement. Know what I mean? No room for slack. He'd be here to tell you that himself but... well, he had to take off early today."

Is that cream cheese on his tie? Jesus, what a slob. So that's what ties are for. Huh. Stopping slobs from soiling their hundred-dollar silk shirts. But I'm not a slob. So why in God's name am I wearing a tie again? I should just take the fucking thing off. I've always hated this one anyway. Looks like a clown threw up on it.

"Bucky!"

"Huh?"

He's quiet now. Finally I can concentrate on just fucking breathing. All his talking and talking and talking. And that smell. God. Is he done yet? Well, he's going to the door. But this is his office. He can't just leave me here. I might kill myself. Well, there's comfort in knowing that then it'd at least be quiet.

"Come on. Jennifer's got a box on your desk. It... doesn't look like you've got much, so... You can grab your personal things and I'll walk you to your car."

"I—My car isn't here. I walked."

"Walked? Buck, that's... that's gotta be, what, ten miles?"

Is it that far? I shrug.

"Look, I-I'll drive you home, okay? Or wherever you want to go."

The office door's open. I think this means I can leave now. Oh, thank Christ. That's just what I'll do. Already the air from the hallway smells better.

"Bucky? Buck. Buck! Come on, I'll drive you."

Fuck him. I've got nothing here worth keeping. I don't even want my coat. Would just smell like this place for ages after I'm gone. Gone. Huh. It feels good to think that. I'm gone. Out of here. I'm never coming back. This is it.

I almost feel like skipping down the hall and through the reception doors like a goddamn schoolboy after the last bell. But I don't. I let my access card flop to the floor, and I push open the double doors. I hear a few of them behind me, calling out their "see yas" and "take cares," but who are they bullshitting? I won't be seeing them and they won't be seeing me. And what do I have worth taking care of anymore?

Fuck this tie. Good riddance.

When did it get so fucking hot out? This morning it was colder than a snowman's dick; now it's hotter than hell. Goddamn New England weather. Is it too much to ask for some consistency for once? Just for a day? Well, at least the sun is out. And no one's talking.

"Excuse me?"

Shit. No. I don't hear you, guy.

"Excuse me! *Excuse! Me!*"

God. Dammit. Maybe if I just look at this asshole, he'll see I'm a nobody and will leave me the fuck alone and keep driving.

Nope. Not working.

"Oh, hey. Do you know where…"

"No."

"… But I didn't say the address yet."

"Not from around here."

"Oh. Well maybe you've heard of—"

"No. Sorry." Time to walk. If this fella is smart, he'll drive away now and not say another fucking word.

There you go. Good boy.

Shit, is it hot. I would've thrown my jacket away, too, if I had it.

Looks like there's a dead cat by the side of the road, up ahead. She's got one of those long coats, too, that annoying, fluffy kind that drags along the ground and makes for massive hairballs. I don't know how animals stand it, having a coat they can never take off, in heat like this. Damn thing is fresh, too. Maybe this heat drove it nuts, and getting flattened by a car was its only source of relief. She just couldn't take it anymore. It was too much. Can't take the heat, might as well get moving. Or… what was it Frank said? "Get hitting the pavement?" You and me both, poor girl. You and me, both. Unlike you, my brains are still on the inside, but I bet they feel just as bad.

What's it been now? Four? Five miles? The sun is just not letting up. Hasn't anyone heard of planting fucking trees along the road? Neighborhood beautification, save the Earth and all that shit? I think I just need to sit down, somewhere out of this godforsaken sun. My choices right now are a bank and a little league field. Or the crumbling sidewalk, I guess. I'd consider the bank outright, if it wasn't for the smell of food from the field.

I thought I wouldn't catch myself dead going back into one of these places again, but right now I just about feel close to death. And, damn it, I'm hungry too.

"What can I get ya?"

"Dog... and a beer."

"Beer? No beer here. This is a little league game."

I'm trying to look disappointed, but I doubt my expression is changing much at all.

The old concession guy leans in. "Can't say what the other folks are bringing into this place in their coolers and whatnot, though. Know what I mean? Eh?" He mimics a drinking motion with a cupped hand.

"Uh. Yeah."

"So a dog and... ? Anything else?"

"Just a water then."

"Alrighty. Eight seventy-five."

Jesus. I hand him two sweaty fives I fish from my pocket. The old coot picks the crumpled bills from the counter like they're radioactive. Whatever. I take the food and the buck he hands back. I leave the quarter.

There's a game going on, but I just need to sit. There aren't a whole lot of people, maybe fifteen or so. Probably all the other parents are still at work.

Work. Shit. I just lost my job, didn't I? A job that paid for this $8.75 sorry example of a meal. The one that paid for all my meals, and the ones after this. But... not anymore. One last paycheck and then that's it. I feel like I should give more of a shit, but I don't really. This'll be the best fucking six-dollar hot dog I ever had. It'll taste free.

Freedom's got to taste glorious.

"Jason! Jason! Look alive, will ya? Don't be hanging back like last time. You see the chance to take a base, you take it, understand?"

Freedom apparently doesn't include not having my ears raped by some douchebag. One of the coaches, I'm guessing. I can't see his face, but I can sure hear the shit it's expelling. He's ripping into one of the kids. Said kid, Jason, has got both feet on first base, looking up as a helicopter flies by overhead. Despite the asshole he's got to listen to, he looks like he's enjoying himself. Good boy.

"Ah, man. JASON!"

Please. Please just shut the fuck up. Leave the fucking kid alone.

I look at the half-eaten hot dog in my hand. What the hell am I doing here?

I can't hear the crack of a bat, but the reaction of the people around me some kid made a hit. Jason's still in whatever world his head is in. It's just not this one right now.

Some woman's yelling to my right. "Run! Come on, run! Go!"

The ball is somewhere near third base. Infielders are scrambling around for it. And the batter is not slowing down. He and Jason are a ball of dirt and dust on first. Jason lands three feet away, face-down, next to his hat. The first baseman catches the throw, tags the poor kid eating mud. He's looking around like he doesn't know what hit him. Half the stands are groaning; the other is half-assedly applauding. I'm finishing my hot dog.

"JASON! The dugout! Now!" It's that asshole again. He's really getting on my nerves. And now my tie feels tight again. Only I'm not wearing one. Damn. Where the fuck's my water?

There's tapping on my back. "Hey. Dropped this."

"Huh?"

"Here." The guy behind me hands me my water. Must've fallen off the bench.

"Thanks."

"Which one's yours?"

My mouth's full of water. "Hm?"

He points to the dugouts. "Your boy with the Badgers or the Trojans?"

"... Trojans?"

"Trojans. Ah! You guys are four-and-oh. Tough team."

"Oh. Yeah."

"Nice we could get out early to see 'em play."

I nod and keep drinking. A pop fly's caught, and the field clears. Jason's wiping his face with the back of his glove and heading toward right field. The son-of-a-bitch coach made the poor kid cry. For being a kid.

Water-boy behind me claps his hands a few times. "All right, David! Nice catch! Good inning, guys!" He leans forward. "Sorry. That's my son."

I have nothing to say to that.

"I'm Paul Gordon, by the way. This is Sally."

Oh, for crying out loud. Can I just tell Paul and Sally to fuck off right now? Would that be an okay thing to do? I'm thinking probably not. I should probably answer him. It probably won't make him go away, but maybe if I speak with my back turned...

"Buchanan. Fairchild."

He's quiet. Thank Christ, I think it worked.

"Wait... Fairchild? Buchanan Fairchild, not like... Bucky Fairchild?"

Oh, fucking fantastic. I should've known. "Junior," I say.

"Ho-ly... Sally, you know who this is? This is Bucky Fairchild's kid! Man. I grew up watching your father. Holy crap, he knew how to hit. I got to see a game once at Fenway, and your father sailed one ten feet over the Green. I'll never forget it."

"Yup. He was a hard hitter all right."

"So... what about you? You a ball player now?"

Just stop. *STOP!* Stop. Talking! I'm going to say it. I swear to God I'm going to say it.

"Nope. Got a, uh, bad arm."

"Aw, shit. That sucks. Sorry to hear that. Accident?"

No, you nosy, insensitive prick! You want to hear about how my father nearly tore my right arm off my torso when I failed to catch a fly ball he hit my way? How he continued to turn and turn until my shoulder popped? And even then, when whatever sick lesson he was trying to teach me was done being taught, and while I screamed and pleaded for him to please stop stop STOP hurting me, he kept on twisting. We told Mom and the hospital that I hurt it falling out of the treehouse. I couldn't move it at all for over a year. I was never good at throwing with my left, and I never tried. I was done. No, you don't want to hear that. No one wants to hear that. You and everyone else wants to hear about the great hero, the man who could do no wrong and who'd never lay a finger on another living soul, much less his own wife and son. It's the only thing you'll accept.

"Yeah."

"Well... I'm sorry about him passing away. Five years ago and all, but I still wanted to pass on my respects."

Respects. For him. There's only so much laughter I can contain. "Sure. Appreciate it."

"At least you've got your boy in there, right? Well, uh, where... did you say your kid was again?"

Just go the fuck away. Please just leave me alone. I should be sitting in that god damn bank right now.

"Uh. Right there." I point out the pitcher. Stupid.

"Who? Derek? Isn't that Randy's kid?"

Shit. "Huh? Oh, uh, no. That's him, there. Right field." There's Jason, already busy counting dandelions on the field. Sweet kid.

Sounds like that shut Paul up. Hopefully it's not because Jason is another kid he happens to know.

This time I hear the hit. It's solid. A popper to right field, clear over the head of my boy. Of course, he's oblivious.

"JASON! Wake up!" It's that ball-busting coach again. I've about had enough of him. "JA-SON! Get. The. BALL! MOVE!"

Jason's head is up, but it's too late. The centerfielder has it. He lobs it back to the mound, since the batter's already safe on second. Parents of Badgers cheer; Trojans groan. Except for me. I'm clapping my fool hands off, because, hey, that's my goddamn boy out there. "Looking sharp, Jason!"

Paul's leaning in again. "I thought you said your son's name was Jason."

"Huh? What did I say?"

"You said 'Jeremy.'"

Bullshit. "Uh. No I didn't."

"Yeah. You did."

A few heads are turning to look, with expressions that question whether I'm kidding or not. Fuck them all. No, I am not kidding. Come on, the kid's enjoying himself. That's what the fuck it's all about! That's what life is about, you pretentious dicks.

Jason's looking up to the stands, his eyes shielded from the sun with his glove. I give him a wave. I'm his dad, after all. Hello, son. It's me. Go on; keep eyeing the weeds, kid.

Thought I'd feel better by now, but I feel like shit. My stomach's in fucking knots. Probably that sorry excuse for a hot dog. The water's gone right threw me. And this goddamn heat. How are those kids playing in this shit?

Well, I drained every last drop from the bottle. Now I've got an urgent need to go drain myself.

Bathrooms aren't too far. Not surprisingly, it smells like bleach and stale piss. At least I'm alone. Sweet relief. Outside, there're more cheers and groans. They die off as someone steps up to the urinal beside me.

"Hey."

Fantastic. Another talker. I just won't say anything.

"God, what a painful inning."

His voice. I know it. Fuck, I know this voice. It's for sure the jerk-off coach who's been screaming at the kids all day, but not that's not all. Randal Chapman. Up until a couple of hours ago he was two heads up the totem pole from me. Of course it would be him. There's at least some solace in knowing he keeps to the golden rule of men's room etiquette: eyes forward. He doesn't see who I am. Last on my list of things I wanted to do today was talking to—

"Bucky? What... ? Uhm. What are you doing here, Buck?"

"Watching my son play. He's with the, uh, Badgers." I flush and head to the sinks. I need to get the fuck out of here.

"Really, I... I didn't know you had another kid."

"What?" Another kid? What the hell is he talking about?

"Well, I... just that, well, what was his name? Jeremy? Jeffrey? Figured he was all you had."

What the fuck is going on? God, what is it? I feel like I could throw up. The smell? Listening to Chapman chew my ear off again? He flushes and stands at the other sink.

"Well, whatever. So I gather that Frank gave you the news. Y'know, with you being here and all. I didn't want it to have to go down that way, Buck."

Deep breaths. Deep. Breaths. Let the cold sweats pass. Swallow down that choking lump. You can do this. You can.

"It's been a tough year so far. Last quarter was for shit. Had to let four go then, too, remember? I didn't want to have to do it. In fact, I didn't do it. They did it to themselves. I know, I know. I'm always the bad guy in all of this, but I'm not the one deciding who's bringing in the dollars, know what I mean? You guys all decide that for yourselves. And you know we're not all bad guys, Bucky. We make concessions all the time, like for you with... well, with what happened with your son. But we can only do so much of it for so long. Then it's back to doing what you're here to do. Get your head back in the game. You hit hard or—"

"You hit the pavement." I've heard this one.

"Right. Right. It's a shame you had to do the latter." He pats me on the back. Bastard didn't dry his hands.

"Get your fucking hand off me."

"What? Excuse me?"

"I said get your hand off me, you heartless piece of shit!" Deep. Breaths.

"Heartless? Oh, really. Now you—"

"Hey, Randy!" It's Paul. Can I not get rid of this guy? "Your boy Derek gonna ease up on us out there a little or what? Hey, Bucky."

Randal looks stunned. "Bucky? Paul, you know this guy?"

"Well, we just met, but yeah, this is Bucky Fairchild. Sorry: Junior."

"Fairchild? What, like the ball player?" Randal doubles over with laughter. "Bucky Fairchild Junior? He wishes!"

I think I'm about to pass out. Don't pass out. Inhale. I cannot pass out. Exhale.

"I don't get it," Paul says.

"This guy works—sorry—*worked* for me. We just let him go. His name's Buchanan *MacGowan*. He wishes his father was Bucky Fairchild, I can tell you that. *This* Bucky's father: you know who he is?"

Paul shakes his head.

My legs feel like limp noodles. "Shut up, Randal."

"No, no. Let me finish. This guy's father is Dick Mac-Gowan. *The* Richard MacGowan. Ring a bell? It was just last year."

"Jesus."

"Right? Named his son here after his favorite ball player. At least the first name. You got the first part of it, but you're stuck with the soiled-up last. Isn't that right, Buck?"

Paul backhands Randal on the chest. "Randy. C'mon, man."

It's dark in here. Is it that late already? I need to get outside. I can't stand another second next to these putrid stalls, listening to Randal-fucking-Chapman. And I'm certainly not going to puke in front of them.

I lean into the barrel outside and fill it with half-digested hot dog, water, and bile. I'm not sure I feel any better. It's so fucking hot out here. Aren't there more buttons I can undo on this shirt? Fuck it. It can join the hot dog. Just a t-shirt's fine. I can hear those two still squawking in the bathroom behind me.

"Randy, you can sometimes be a cruel bastard, you know that?"

"Oh, please! You should've heard how he was talking back to me before you came in. Like he's better than me. Yeah. Well, let me tell you: he's a primetime loser. He's no different than the dozen or so pieces of trash I had to let go in the past month. They just don't step up to the plate. They don't. Hit. *Hard.* They become cannon fodder. And then he comes here to, what, tell me off? For telling him the God's-honest truth? So now he's got a set of balls, and that's how he uses them? Fuck him."

"But... the guy lost his son, for crying out loud."

Jeremy.

"Come on, Paul. Really? That was six months ago. How long does the guy need that crutch to hold him up, huh? What, like, a year? It wasn't until last week he stopped camping out in front of his son's damn crypt for hours all day, instead of closing sales. The company can't afford that."

Dad, stop! Dad, you're going to hurt him again!

"You shut the hell up, Bucky! You're teaching this boy of yours that it's okay to slack off. Like his father."

He's just being a kid! He doesn't want to play the stupid game your way! Let him be!

"Are you seriously talking back to me, boy? Because it sure sounds like you are. You may be old enough to sprout kids, but you're still a chicken-shit little boy to me. I'm finally let out, and then I come home to more of this shit? Do I need to teach you another lesson too? Huh? Maybe take that other shoulder of yours, make them match?"

STOP!

"Not like you're using them for no good no more."

Stop it! Shut up!

"Just stay in the house, Bucky. Do something useful and bring me another fucking beer. You! J.B.! Step up to the plate! NOW!"

Dad! He's done! He doesn't want to play!

"You dodge this pitch again, boy, and I will take that bat to your puny skull, you understand me?"

"No! Daddy! DADDY! Tell him I don't wanna! He throws them too fast!"

Jeremy! It's okay, Jeremy! I'm coming! DAD! STOP!

"Here's. The. PITCH!"

"Jeremy!"

Jeremy. He's gone. He took Jeremy from me. Took him from everyone, from the world. Took him from everything he wanted to do and everything he ever wanted to be. He wasn't even old enough to know what that was yet. Because he didn't need to.

"Bucky? Bucky, you okay, man?"

"Leave him alone, Paul. Let him get it out of his system. Then maybe he can get on with his life and make a goddamn difference."

I didn't want to remember. It was easier that way. To live life, if this is what living a life is supposed to be. But it's not. I'm not fooling anyone, and I can only fool myself for so long. But I'm tired of it. This isn't who I am, and it's not who I'm going to be. I can't forget anymore. I won't forget. Now I can be who I'm supposed to be.

There are too many pieces of shit in this toilet of a world telling me to be someone I am not.

My knuckles are a mess. How long have I been sitting here punching at pieces of sidewalk?

"Jason! God *DAMMIT!* Jason!"

There he goes. Even from here, I can hear him.

"Jason! Off the field! NOW! Brian, you take his spot. Jason and I need to have a little talk."

I'm on my feet now. Feels good. I can breathe again. And I've got what I need. It fits just right in my hand. Paul's coming down from the stands as I walk by. "Bucky. Jesus, man. Your hands. You all right?"

Not now, Paul.

Randal's face is inches away from the boy's. He's got the front of the kid's shirt balled up in his hand. "Jason, I swear to God, if you don't—"

"Randal!"

He lets go and turns to face me. "MacGowan? Well, what the hell do you want now? Can't you see I'm in the middle of something?"

"It's time to step up to the plate."

"What?"

"Step up to the plate, *boy*!"

"Are you nuts? Get the hell off my field!"

There's one good thing I can say about this heat: my shoulder hasn't bothered me all day. In fact, it feels... fantastic.

"Remember what you've always said, Randal? You've got to hit hard."

"Jesus, you really are nuts. Your loony father really rubbed off on you."

"Uhm. Coach?" says the kid. "Who's that?"

The fingers of my right hand close around the broken piece of sidewalk just right. It feels heavy, feels good.

"Will you shut it, Jason? Can't you see that—"

It feels even better when my fingers part and I let the heater fly.

"Get your head in the game!" I say.

It's a hit. Strike three. Final out.

Look at that. He looks a bit like that cat now. Just could not take the heat.

"You hit it hard or you get hitting the pavement, Randal. Isn't that right?"

And the crowd goes wild.

HALLO-WHEN

While Saint Ambrose exists as a resting place for the deceased, it is a poor receptacle for storing memories of bygone lives. A placard or tombstone serves no further purpose than a name tag for passersby to observe, perhaps appended with a phrase or two of accomplishments and endearments; to the memory of the person who lies beyond or below these words, they but scratch the surface. Memories of them remain with those who live on. Whether they choose—or are able—to recall them is another matter, one they must live with until their time comes as well.

What of those who have passed, one wonders? Do memories of who they once were in life continue beyond mortality? Are they as free to choose to forget, just as the living might, or are they forever reminded of their past? I suppose it all depends on what one believes of the afterlife. Can the aging mind of a soul deteriorate just as that of the living? Unlikely, I would say.

For the living, it is a biological certainty that, in time, memories fade. By the time one enters their twilight years, they find themselves forgetting all manner of things.

Of people: "Sally-who?"

Places: "Saint-where?"

Even moments in time: "Hallo-when?"

———◦———

Bill left the den air conditioner on again. I'm sure I will never understand why that man insists it be as cold as an icebox on the North Pole every blessed moment in this house. And my lord is it noisy. The quiet night air is just fine without it this time of year, so off it goes.

Well. He will just have to settle with being a tad "stuffy," as I seem to recall him putting himself. Better stuffy than catching your death, I say.

It's just as well, with him busying himself with lord-knows-what in the cellar again while I'm left to my lonesome upstairs alone.

Lonesome. I can't say why, but I feel as though I should be saddened by the thought. I love Bill dearly and all, but the man can be quite nonsensical at times. *Most* times that I can recall, I say. An enigma, he is. Never can understand him.

There is what sounds to be a light knock on the porch door. At first I think the sound to be Bill again, messing with his doo-dads and what-nots in that hellish place down below. But sure as snowflakes, there it is again. A light tap-tapping sound, just outside.

I think to myself, *What an odd hour for a visitor*. Here, at the end of this farm road that's sure to be a clear half-mile long. A neighbor, perhaps? I hope they're all right. It is quite late.

Bill usually likes to answer to visitors these days, so I wait for him to head on up. But, again, the knocking, and I'd say with a fair level of some insistence for an answer now.

Oh, to Hell with Bill.

I call out, "Coming!" as the last knock falls.

Though the porch light is on, its door is without windows, so I cannot see who might be outside. I think to open it before my wits overcome me.

"Who is it?" I ask.

It seems a dog's age before there's a reply.

"T-Trick. Or. T-Treat."

I cover my mouth to stifle a laugh, and I shake my head in sheer disappointment in myself for having not known what day it was. Of all the blessed days of the year, how could I have forgotten that today was Halloween? I've had no time for decorations! No candy! Why, no costume of my own! How could Bill have not reminded me? That scoundrel of a man.

Without further hesitation, I pull the door open to its widest. There on the front porch is a solitary figure: a child, who couldn't be but ten. A little girl, or so I believe, as her costume is by far and wide one to behold.

"T-Trick—"

"Oh, would you look at you!" I exclaim. "That is a scary costume you have there. So... gruesome!"

And indeed it is gruesome. Delightfully so. While she wears an adorable blue fairytale-like dress with a white smock, it is near-fully soiled by soot and costume blood. The mask she wears is indeed a terrifying sight, the appearance of what was once a beautiful girl now a ruin of flesh and bone so much as to be unrecognizable. There is only but one eye I can see, precariously dangling from what appears to be fine thread. Only half of what would be gorgeous locks of golden hair cover her head, the rest a mass of reddened scalp beneath exposed skull. An elaborate piece that, I must say, I do admire.

"Tr—"

Her speech is but a gurgle, what with all the flesh parts of her mask covering her mouth.

"It's a wonder you can speak! Tell me, did your folks help you put that together? Your mum?"

At this she falls silent. Her breath ragged. Only her empty bag hangs open before her. It, too, as soiled as her garb.

"Oh my goodness. I'm so embarrassed. Sorry, my... mind is not so sharp these days. I don't have any—"

But I do. I do, and I may just about jump for joy if I could at the recollection. I hold out a finger of wait to the girl and rush back inside.

Bill has forever had a sweet tooth. I and his dentures could not forget this unfortunate fact. Reaching the kitchen, I open his cabinet nearly clear off its hinges and reach inside. A Hershey's chocolate bar. It's the only one left, with two squares already taken. I suppose I will just fault Bill for not thinking so clearly himself, in that it is he who's kept his own stock so light and will now have to go without.

I arrive back to the porch. The girl remains, seemingly swaying to an unsung song, patiently awaiting her bounty. Her costume, it appears, has gotten the best of the remains of her dress, it now more red than not.

"Here we are. I'm so sorry, it's... opened. My husband has a way with candy, I guess you could say. Hope you don't mind."

I place Bill's last bit of indulgence into the girl's bag, careful as I can not to have it covered in the mess that continues to issue from her mask.

"*M... M...*"

She speaks, but for the life of me I can't make sense of what she is trying to say. But there... is something...

"Where did you come from, dear? Where are your folks?"

"*M... M...*"

Again, there is... something. My mind. God damn, my mind. "Have I... seen you around before, sweetie?"

I'm not sure what I've done to cause it, but she turns and walks away. Down the porch steps. Down the pebbled driveway. Out into the night, a night cold enough to bring my own breath to a fog before me. Much too cold for air conditioning, and far too dark for a little girl to rightfully be traveling in alone.

I motion to call out. I stop something that compels me to run off after her. If there is nothing else I know, it is that my frail, Godforsaken legs would not carry me far, least of all down the stairs.

Just as I close the door, Bill is in the kitchen. He'd come up, and I hadn't noticed.

"Irene?!"

At first, I don't answer. There is something within me that has something to say yet... it just will not come. Something.

"Irene. Did you eat my Hershey's?"

"No, Bill. I... Bill, why didn't you tell me it was Halloween?"

"What?"

"Halloween! *Halloween!* You didn't... you didn't think to remind me it was Halloween!"

"Halloween? Well, what gave you that idea?"

"There was..."

Bill's concerned. He has that face again. He doesn't care about the chocolate anymore and comes into the living room, pulls me into his big arms. He smells like the old boxes of things we store our photographs and memories in. Sometimes the entire house smells like him. Sometimes—like now—I think I like it.

"Honey. Honey. Halloween. I know. Your favorite... holiday, you used to call it. Used to wonder why the station didn't give me the day off."

"It... was my favorite day, wasn't it?" I say. And then I remember. "It *is* my favorite day."

He laughs a little, like he's remembering something too.

"You could say that, yep. Used to have this whole place decked out in spiderwebs. Had me play scary music from the stereo. Lord knows nobody came up to this neck of the woods for candy, but that didn't stop you."

He laughs again, but it seems different now. "You used to dress up to scare the Devil himself, I swear. Last time... Lord, it was so long ago. I think I recall you and Bonnie dressed up as fairytale characters. You were... Oh! You were the Mad Hatter, only with his head cut off. You held a bloody melon with a hat in your hands! You were mad, all right! But not Bonnie, she—"

"Bonnie?"

His hug gets tight. It feels good, but I know there's something not quite right.

"Yeah," he says, and swallows hard in my ear. "She... she just wanted to be Alice in Wonderland. Nothing scary. Just... so pretty."

"Who's Bonnie?"

Bill pulls away and hides his face from me, wiping cellar grime from his face and eyes.

"Our girl, Irene. Our Bonnie. After all these years, I still miss her. I can barely get my fat arse in the truck these days, to go out to Saint Ambrose, place some flowers where she's laid to rest. Heck, it's why I'm downstairs all the time, looking at the old pictures we have of her instead. And today... today, of course..."

"Halloween?"

He laughs, sounding a bit more like himself. "Today she would have been forty years old. Her birthday. *Forty*, can you believe that? Christ, are we old." He holds me again.

"Twenty-nine years," he says. "I thought I'd lost you both."

He lets me go and starts into the den. I still can make no sense on what he's going on about.

"Y'know, there aren't a whole lotta blessings I can come up with these days, but there are three in particular that help me sleep at night."

"What's that?" I ask.

"Well. One—and sorry to have to admit this—that the accident made you unable to ever drive again. And two, that... horrible thing you went through the last time you drove... with Bonnie... it did something to your mind where you can't remember what happened to our little girl. Sometimes I envy you of that. And I thank God you're mostly okay."

Little girl. Bonnie. I feel at any moment my Bill is going to hop right into the Halloween spirit unlike he'd ever done and tell me this is all some scary story—some awful, awful nightmare of a story—and that Halloween is as special of a time to him as it's ever been to me.

"And the third?" I ask. "What's that?"

He presses the button on the air conditioner, and the silence of the night is as gone as my recollection of why we are having such an odd conversation in the first place.

"Air conditioning. Sweet, sweet AC. My god is it stuffy. It's the middle of July, Irene."

PLACEMENT

*I*n Saint Ambrose, each resident has their place—be it among the polished marble vaults or in the well-worn pages of memory. But sometimes, the placement of the living is as precarious as that of the departed. The choices of where one belongs—be it in the service of others or in the sanctuary of faith—carry consequences heavier than any stone laid to rest here.

Father Quinn, a man of unwavering conviction, always believed his place was in the arms of God, serving as a shepherd to his flock. But conviction has a way of being tested in Saint Ambrose. What happens when one's sense of duty blinds them to the shadows creeping closer? What price must be paid when devotion becomes obsession, and the line between protector and prisoner begins to blur?

Yes, in Saint Ambrose, even the most faithful must reckon with their choices. For some, the greatest struggle is not finding their place—but keeping it.

So pour one out, as they say, to Father Quinn, for his steadfast resolve could not escape the immense weight of placement.

—◆◇◆—

Fading, crimson legs of a 2012 Beaujolais made their descent along the interior of Quinn's glass, the pool of wine settling from a casual swirl and welcoming them downward home. The priest nodded somewhat appreciatively as its finish lingered in his mouth.

Perhaps a tad too fruit-forward for my tastes. But it's decent for a change.

The blurry visage of the chessboard loomed at him from beyond the wine bowl.

"It's your move, Father," Joseph said.

Quinn frowned and nodded whilst fingering the delicate silver crucifix dangling from his neck. Behind him, an icy wind howled and threw itself upon the window. This was not the wet snow from the week prior. This was ice in its purest form, obliterated into particles within the atmosphere and cast onto the world as a blanket of ill comfort. The sound of it alone drove Quinn to shiver, for it was as though death itself called to him for entry.

"Father?"

Quinn waved a dismissive hand. "Yes, yes. I know it's my move. You said so already."

"No, it's not that. I mean... it's about my placement, Father."

Quinn's frown grew.

"Has there been—"

"I understand it can be frustrating, Joseph," the priest interrupted. "As you know, placement takes time."

"I do know, Father. It's just that... well, what I mean is... is this where I'm meant to stay? Where I'm meant to end up, after all this time? Is this home?"

Quinn studied the chessboard a moment before he spoke. "I believe every one of you deserves a place to call home. I do not by any means consider this to be the place you 'end up,' as you put it."

"I know. I do. But it sure feels that way sometimes."

Quinn reached out and snagged a black rook between two fingers, sliding it across the empty first row, four spaces to the left, stopping beside the black king. The king he then placed to the other side of the rook.

Joseph craned his neck to inspect the move. "Castling. Again."

Quinn relaxed back into his chair. "What can I say? It's always been my go-to."

A light knock came at the closed door from across the room. Joseph glanced over his shoulder at the noise, then, with some worry, to the priest. Quinn drained the rest of the wine from his glass as both men stood. He motioned to the open door to his right.

"Carry on, Joseph. God be with you. You'll be placed before you know it." He turned to the window, his breath casting a fog upon it barely contrasting against the palette of white outside. "On days like this... I have high hopes for many of you."

Joseph nodded. He left through the open door, into the milling group of the others at the Saint Ambrose House, deprived of a place to call home.

Delicate taps again at the closed door. Quinn corked the wine. The bottle and glass went into the bottom drawer of his desk. He had so been looking forward to enjoying more of it. There were not many opportunities for a patron of the homeless to partake in such lavishness. What would someone think, were they to see him? Waving the sins of habit and addiction under the noses of those so easily weakened and tempted by material spoils of the world. *How dare you. You are a man of God! What were you thinking?* What did they know of material spoils? The meandering souls under his care at Ambrose could not care less whether or not he was spilling wine down his gullet or plunging pleasure into a vein. They'd of course rather he chose the former, as it was less dangerous, but they were a selfish lot. They'd much rather he stuck around a bit more. At least he had something to show for what he'd done for them all.

"Come in."

The door opened just enough for Sister Estelle's head to poke through. Her look darted about the room as though it were empty. After a moment, she fully entered, clothed neck-to-feet in an over-abundance of sub-zero garb.

Quinn slumped back into his chair. "So this is it, then. You're leaving us."

Shame flushed the Sister's face. "I'm sorry, Father. Yes, I think it's best for, um… for everyone. I… don't think I'm suited to do this anymore. Or perhaps ever was, if I'm being perfectly honest."

"I see." He removed his glasses and began cleaning them with a cloth from the desk. He smirked; the pun was not lost on him. "All of them deserve a home, Sister. This shelter is merely a temporary stopping point. I'm tasked with having to place them."

"I understand that, Father, but—"

"If my methods unsettle you, then be on your way."

She flinched at the priest's abruptness. "So… that's it, then? You're just going to let me leave? No more convincing? You've nothing more to say?"

"If I couldn't convince you in all this time, Sister, I certainly am doing no good for either of us to try doing it again now. Your mind's made up; that much is clear."

"I see. Well, right you are, then. Thank you, Father. Thank you… for everything." She pulled the door with her as she retreated back out of the room.

"Oh, uh, Sister Estelle."

"Yes, Father?"

"On your way out, if you'd be so kind as to put the kettle on? I feel the cold has seeped into my bones at this point, and a hot cup calls out to me."

"Of course."

"Thank you, Sister. And, truly, I wish you well. Godspeed."

With that, the nun completed her exit.

At the other office door stood another woman. Clearly, she was no nun. Her slinky red dress hung loose off thin shoulders. It was a dress suited for someplace much richer and warm, and she wore it with the comfort of such a place. Loops of pearls draped over her neck under curls of golden hair. Diamond bracelets rounded her wrists. The sight of her alone drove the priest to chills. But he knew why she'd come. It was why any of them had come. Without a word, his permissive look gave her what she'd come for.

Though delivered with warmth, her smile hit Quinn cold.

Like Laura's mother, winter was a cold, cruel, heartless, un-forgiving, and unrelenting bitch. Laura can think of many more ways to describe her feelings for both, but they are much too kind for her mother and much too cruel for the snow. There was a time when Laura Mills found winter to be lovely. About her mother, she was rather certain she could not say the same.

Winter was kind before Laura Mills became Honey. Father had always called her that, before her mother took him from her and the rest of the world. It left Mother with a punishment that befitted her, and Laura—then, Honey—someplace she couldn't remain. These days, alone was much better; alone and frozen was not.

Laura stomped her snow-caked, sneakered feet upon the only bare spot of sidewalk she could find. It'd been cleared away mostly by the wind, then left damp with the rancid urine of some bum that hadn't yet frozen into a shallow, yellowish-brown slush. That smell was something she'd long gotten used to, and it was better to clear her feet upon it than to not feel her feet at all.

The streets were empty. Of cars and people and anything else alive and moving, but not of the snow. It piled smooth and high, showing only the smallest of indentations where the sidewalk and the pavement met. Hulking, white mounds stood alongside covered parking meters, under which automobiles lay abandoned, awaiting their returning owners like kenneled dogs. It flew about in the air in every direction. Every bit of it seemed to find Laura's uncovered face.

There was some other movement ahead. Contrasting deeply against the stark backdrop, a nun hurried down the stairs of a building a block ahead. Upon reaching the second step, she leaped over the last, into the foot of snow upon the sidewalk. Like Gene Kelly in the rain, she twirled on the spot, arms spread wide and face turned to the sky. This was happiness. Freedom, perhaps. Laura had felt that way for a short time once. It was only once, but there was no mistaking it.

The nun completed her joyous pirouette and began a slow trudge down the sidewalk, away from Laura and her piss-stinking shoes. Laura didn't bother to call out to her—her voice would only become swallowed up by the snow. She knew well enough that seeing the nun meant ahead was a church or shelter, and knowing that was enough. It meant food. It meant warmth. In her current situation, she hoped it meant so much more.

Laura's persistent, desperate knocks touched hard upon the shelter's door. Upon its rusty hinges it opened in a rush, and the girl fell into the building along with intruding clouds of cold and snow.

"Oh, Jesus, thank God!" She looked up, her eyes meeting the spectacled eyes of the middle-aged priest. "Oh my God, I mean, oh my... I'm sorry, Father. I didn't mean—"

Quinn smiled and waved her off. "Don't worry about it. I say 'Jesus' and 'God' all the time. Especially in weather like this."

The girl coughed a relieved laugh. "No kidding."

Quinn shoved the door closed and latched its lock. "So I take it you need a place out of the cold for some time, hm?"

"Oh, hell yes!" She winced. "I mean..."

"I say that word, too. Well, you're lucky. It's quite busy here this time of year, but we'll certainly find a spot for you." The priest extended his right hand. "I'm Father Quinn."

"Honey." She removed the mitten from her right hand and shook his.

"Honey. Well isn't that an interesting name."

A whistling noise grew, sounding far off and through empty rooms and hallways. The two turned in its direction.

"Oh. Someone put on some tea?"

"Coffee, actually. Can't get much better than instant in this place, I'm afraid."

"Ugh. Sorry. Can't stand coffee. Me? I'm a tea girl. Oh, or hot chocolate."

"Ah. Well, I guess I... forgot it was put on. Please, have a seat in my office over here and get comfortable. I'll be back shortly." Quinn hurried down the hallway, out of sight. Laura turned and entered the office.

Besides the brown-paneled walls and a large but otherwise rather nondescript desk and chair, the room was rather bare. Lit only by a solitary window and the door she entered from, it had a lifeless feeling that crossed over into depressing. Lone shelves along one wall stood empty. A chessboard with pieces sat upon the desk. A cheap, Christ-less crucifix hung on the wall beside a closed door. The room could be deemed unremarkable, had its primary occupant not been a man of the cloth.

Laura pulled the zipper of her decade-old ski parka down through caked snow. Between what fell off her coat and what she shook off her shoes and stringy, auburn hair, the wooden floor at her feet became a sudden puddle of quickly melting slush. She stepped through it without a thought and draped the dripping coat upon the back of the one chair across from the desk. The warmth about the room felt life-giving. With shut eyes she remained standing, hugging herself within it.

It was the kettle whistle's sudden ceasing that brought her to. The absence of all other sound but that of the winds of outside trying to get in was jarring. Greeting her was the topside of the desk and the chessboard. She knew not a thing about the game. Was there some kind of solitaire version of it? Here there was a board in what looked like mid-play, without another to play it with. *Must have been the nun*, she thought. Then again, she knew a thing or two about being alone and of having to remain creative to remain on the survivable side of crazy.

Laura turned and considered the closed door. She presumed it to be a closet, and likely a rather empty one at that, considering the condition of the room it belonged to. She approached and placed her hand on its doorknob. Cold. Though it was clearly an interior door, it felt to be emanating the grip of winter through it. Being the creative mind she was, she took the chance to open it.

Creative minds, as it turns out, are naturally curious ones.

This was not outside. Before Laura stood an open expanse of empty cots, neatly arranged in rows, bathed in a subdued colorful light. There seemed to be over a hundred of them, each one unoccupied and made tight as to bounce a quarter off of. The room was as devoid of people as the beds. Daylight issued from the many tall, stained-glass windows lining opposite walls.

"This is busy?" Carried upon chilled breath, her own quiet words to herself echoed throughout the stark-walled room. "Hello? Father Quinn?"

Laura tugged her sleeves over callused hands. Wet footfalls squeaked as she made her way between the rows of beds, toward an open door at the far end of the room. Each bed she passed, identical to the next, wrapped militaristically within grey woolen blankets upon white sheets, topped with thin pillows.

She crossed the threshold into a small kitchen, meticulous and seemingly little-used. Though clearly from another generation, the refrigerator appeared new, as did the microwave and stove.

Upon the latter sat a steaming teakettle, which was about the only thing evidencing use about the place. A large, circular table dominated the center of the tiled floor, sans accompanying chairs. There, two empty coffee mugs sat, awaiting their fill.

Laura opened the refrigerator. Bare and as clear as from a showroom floor. What's more, it wasn't powered on. No light. No issuance of cold, as subtle as it would have seemed in the already frigid room. No power at all, as it turned out, as evidenced by its cord laying rejected on the floor behind it. Her stomach lurched at the thought of another day without filling it.

Maybe they're all getting take-out? She huffed.

The under-counter drawers she found to have a bit more life to them. Matches. Teabags. Lots of instant coffee. It was of comfort to her to see well-used silverware and cutlery slide about when she opened the drawer closest the stove.

Through the kitchen was another room. Above its doorway, a wooden sign: Common Room. Prior thoughts against curiosity were driven from her mind in an instant, for now she was hearing voices. Real voices. Not the priest but someone else, from the room she hadn't yet entered.

Still, the new room was devoid of people. Still, it was ungodly cold. Tables, chairs, two couches. But no people. A television within the corner of the room was the clear source of sound, tuned to a news broadcast about the continuing storm. A woman meteorologist in a blue winter coat faced the camera, being pelted mercilessly by blowing show. Her microphone's wind shield did little to protect it.

"... say that residents should be making preparations for staying put—indoors—for the next few days. Only leave your homes if absolutely necessary. Shelter is of the utmost importance in these dangerous wind-chill temps..."

Laura approached one of the windows. Her breath fogged upon the glass. Rubbing at it, the glass squeaked, and she looked outside into the growing sea of white. Inside the common room, it only seemed to get colder. But outside, it was clearly death. So where was everyone? Why were the beds empty? The halls clear? The common room deserted?

"Guess nobody has anything in common."

"Actually, we have lots in common here, Honey."

The girl wheeled about, nearly falling over onto a couch. Father Quinn stood occupying the room's single doorway. Curls of steam ascended from two mugs in his hands.

"Holy shit! You normally sneak up on people like that?"

Quinn said nothing, took a sip.

"So... where is everyone? I thought you said you were busy."

"We are. Busiest it's been here in, well, ages really."

Laura straightened, putting her hands into her back pockets. "But the place is deserted."

"Mm. That's because of placement."

"Placement."

"Yes. That's what we've come to call it. This shelter—this room, the beds out there—it only serves as a... depot of sorts, I guess you could say. No one is meant to stay for very long."

"So you're giving them a home, you mean."

The priest considered that for a moment, took another noisy sip, then nodded. "Yes, I guess you could say that."

Laura's face beamed. She walked to face Quinn. "Home. A place to live. Sounds too good to be true."

Behind simpering lips Quinn began to respond, but the paring knife was at the priest's throat before a word spilled from his mouth.

The girl's tone was seething. "You wanna know what I think of home? Home is SHIT! You think I want a home? What kind of home do you think I could have, HUH?"

"It's not—"

She pressed the knife closer to his throat. "Shut up! I don't want you to place me anywhere, *Father*. The only place that'll take me in is the penn in Eastboro. Or, if I'm lucky, Montgomery will take me back in with all the crazies. What I do want—what I *need*—is whatever you've got that's worth more than a goddamn buck around here. How I deal with you is up to how fast you make that happen. Understand?"

Quinn's smile had never left his face. Now it grew into more of an expression of pity for the girl than of amusement. "Oh, Honey."

"What, you think I'm joking around here? What the hell is so funny? And... is that fucking coffee you were bringing me? I told you I can't drink that shit!" The mug sailed from the priest's hand as Laura backhanded it from his grip. Shattered pieces of porcelain flew about the wall amongst splashes of hot, cheap caffeine.

Quinn found speaking difficult through his suppressed laughter. "Oh. Oh, Honey. Or whatever your name really is. You misunderstand me. I'm not trying to place you anywhere. Not yet, at least."

Quinn's look turned to regard somewhere just over the girl's shoulder. She turned. She felt it. As her brain struggled to comprehend what she saw, the cold gripped her. This was not the cold about the room, not the cold of outside. Something much deeper and sharp. The translucent shape behind her began to take on a vague, human form, reaching outward, enveloping her within dark, wispy, frigid sheets. The paring knife clattered to the floor. Laura became numb as her world went dark, her final sensation being that of invasive displacement of her self.

Quinn slurped at his coffee. "I told you I had high hopes today, Joseph. Welcome home."

"Thank you, Father," said the girl.

DOUBLEBREAK

"Check. Told you, Father. That castling move was going to bite you."

"Hm. So you did." Quinn tilted his head back to catch what dregs were left at the bottom of his mug. Bringing it back to the desk, he stared with disappointment into its emptiness. "Sorry about what happened to your coffee, Joseph. Did you want me to make you more?"

The girl waved dismissively.

"Well, we could have something more... celebratory?" The priest opened the bottom desk drawer.

"So what happens now? This, uh... I guess this wasn't exactly what I was looking for."

Quinn placed the wine bottle and two glasses onto the desk. "Beggars can't be choosers, Joseph. Seems to me you were in a bit of a hurry."

"I suppose. Not that I'm not appreciative, mind you. To be honest with you, Father, I'm not sure I could thank you enough. I once thought your price was high, but now? Giving you all the money I had socked away was nothing. Listen, I know you've gotten a lot more from the other placements, and I know you don't hear it very often, but thank you, Father. If there's anything more I can do..."

"As a matter of fact, there is." Quinn filled the two glasses and slid one to his guest. "As you know, we've had two placements today. Sister Estelle was... an unexpected occupant, I suppose you could say. And now she and... well, she and dear Alicia within her, you know, have left. So now I'm here to do this work alone. And, Lord knows, I could use a holiday. Someplace... warm, for once. Sandy beaches and all that."

The girl chuckled, sniffed at the wine, then sipped. "I see. Say no more. There's definitely too much to do around here for just one person. And besides, who's going to keep whooping your ass in chess now that I don't need you to make my moves for me? Begging your pardon, of course."

Quinn lowered his glass and laughed. He stood and walked to the open doorway. Hundreds of forms lay or sat upon the beds or made their way along the paths between them. They were his people. He was theirs. Soon, he hoped, they'd be experiencing corporeal existence again. They would all be free, then. They of their meanderings within a world of limbo, he the remainder of their spoils.

"I wouldn't be so sure of that yet, Joseph. Neither one of us has won yet."

At the window, the cold called to be let in.

ZERO

Well, it seems our time lurking about the mortuary together is about up. You'll have to forgive me; I do tend to blather on, I know. Alas, it's not often I have someone living to speak to, you know. Were the mouths of those within these walls able to bemoan having to endure my tales time and again, they'd have a thing or two to say; of that, I am sure.

This is not to say that I don't have more to tell you. Oh, I most certainly do, and you may hear of them in time. I dare say there will be many more tales to come, so long as I am able to draw a breath. Then I suppose it will be up to my successor, hm? You, perhaps?

As you can see, there remain many more empty places here in the mortuary. What stories might I tell of the future occupants some day? Might you tell one day?

Until the final vault door is shut—until the final plot on the land is filled—there will always be room in Saint Ambrose. Room for people, room for stories. I imagine it will be many years—decades, even—before the register of availability here is exhausted, that the final person has been laid to rest, and Saint Ambrose officially reads an open vacancy of zero.

It was only a matter of time.

"Are we there yet?" came one of the quiet, juvenile voices from the back seat. It was not whiny, merely inquisitive. It was the third time the question had come up in the seven-hour drive, though this coming only within the last two. Perhaps it was the growing anxiety permeating from the front seats as they grew closer to their destination that spelled out welcome to the question.

Are we there yet?

"What is it, honey?" Gerry asked. Kandace, his youngest, had been tugging at his raincoat for the past ten minutes. Until now she hadn't any success in seizing his attention. Where his usual irritation with her persistence would have leaped forward, he'd let the contrasting emotions of the surrounding moment take hold. He crouched down slightly for her whisper.

"Is Danny going to die, Daddy?"

The two stood beside the hospital bed where their only son and brother lay unmoving and unaware, their raincoats still draining of the thunderstorm. Kandace's blond hair of curls was kept perfect and dry by the Hello Kitty umbrella, now folded and adding rainwater to the growing puddles at her booted feet. Gerry's greying hair remained soaked to the scalp, his face glistening with a mix of God's tears and those of his own. He was thankful his little girl couldn't tell the difference.

"He's fighting very hard not to, honey," Gerry said.

He hated the thought of giving his girls false hope when he had none himself. It was a fact that Danny was fighting—and that they were doing what they could to fight alongside him—but there was no reason yet to believe he would fare one way or the other at this point. It was also a fact that, in his current state, Danny was in pain. Gerry was thankful then, too, that his girls had no notice of this.

The machines beside Danny's bed continued their autonomous rhythm, working in their own way to keep Danny alive. Gerry had long forgotten the names of them. In some ways he loathed how something so mechanical and lifeless could sustain a life. At any moment a faceless person could make the decision for them, and the machines' job would end along with the life they were saving. Perhaps it was more that he felt envy.

Who ultimately holds the decision for a life to go on: those permitting it, or those providing it?

"Not quite, honey," Gerry answered. Somehow his tone was calm, not at all irritated, not worried nor further heightening the feeling of angst already quite well saturating the air around the four. Seven hours was long for any trip, especially one with no stops beyond the requisite pit stop for fuel. There was no time for potty. For those who couldn't wait for a necessary pause for a gas station fill-up or line of traffic, it was into an empty water bottle or Tupperware they went, then that out the window and over the side. That was the rare time traffic was welcome.

The four now sat in the kind of highway stoppage so persistent that a driver could tend to relent, resting the car's engine rather than expend precious fuel to provide the comforts of warmth or cooling for its passengers. Cooling, this time, being the key element of relief. The outside temperatures leveled at ninety degrees at that hour, though the SUV's interior felt closer to one hundred. In reality, it was ten above that.

Gerry's wife, Ruth—the quiet voice's mother—reached from the passenger seat to turn on the car's radio once more.

"Hey," her husband said, stopping her and gently taking hold of her wrist. "The engine's off. You might kill the battery turning that on."

"We need to know what's going on," Ruth said. Sounding unfazed by surrounding circumstances was not a strength she carried. "We've been stopped here for a half-hour. We need to know if we're close enough. To be sure." She left the last sentence softer than the rest, meant this time for his ears alone.

Gerry had the same bothering question for the past hour, though he kept it to himself. He was good at being unreadable. "Not yet," he said. "Look, they're moving."

A quarter-mile ahead, where the road dipped and turned around a center island of rock and birch, the unbroken line of cars began to separate and advance. Others around them, too, saw the change in scenery. The sound of ignitions turning over brought the children upright in their seats.

"They're moving!" repeated Lisa, the other little one from the back. Their own car awoke as well, the air conditioning once again exhaling to life. The issuing blast at first covered the passengers in a wave of once-suppressed aridness, quickly tamed by the influx of freon-cooled air.

Gerry sat forward in his chair with his forearms propped across his thighs. His loosened tie dangled off his neck and between his legs, motionless despite his right heel's nervous drumming against the floor. From his pants pocket, his phone vibrated in announcement of an incoming call; it would've reminded him that his lunch break was long over, if he'd been less preoccupied to notice it. Seated to his left, Ruth reached over and touched his back in a gesture of reassurance, her hand clammy from being clasped within her other for what felt like hours.

From the other side of the ornate desk they were facing, Doctor Anthony Parks opened another folder. Unlike the others—yellow and close to bursting, overstuffed with printouts of charts, forms and logs—this held but one sheet of paper. The folder's red color and the delicate, deliberate way the doctor handled it spelled out the importance of its singular contents. The doctor considered the document a long moment before lifting his eyes above his reading glasses. He placed the paper on his desk, turned it, and slid it between the two visitors seated across from him.

Gerry snatched the paper before his wife could react, and she leaned in for a look. "What is this?" Gerry asked the doctor.

"It's the rest of your son's life, Gerry."

"Tony, this looks like the same treatment Danny's been getting for the past year," Gerry said, his eyes hitting upon words like "neuroregeneration" and "CSPGs." They held little meaning to him but were nonetheless familiar.

"Mostly, that's true. But you know as well as I do that it's doing no good. You saw for yourself that Danny's holding on, but his quality of life is... well, it's declining quickly. I'm sorry I can't candy-coat it much more than that. If we're going to continue down this route, we can't just keep up the current regimen: we need to intensify it."

"*Intensify* it?" Gerry blurted out in disbelief and blindly handed the page to his wife. "Have you really seen Danny lately? This shit you're giving him has sucked the life out of him. He looks worse than he did the day after the accident, and he feels worse too. Jesus, Tony, the kid's eighteen years old and has permanent wrinkles on his face from straining in pain every damned day for nearly a year."

The doctor held his hands up in an effort to calm his friend. "I know, Gerry. No one said it was going to be an easy road. For Danny, we can continue to keep him sedated throughout the treatment and, like always, hope for the best. But it's all I've got for you right now."

Gerry's eyes drifted downward, partly in thought though mostly in regret for having lashed out at the man who was, at that moment, blameless.

"Is there any chance he'll come out of this, Tony?" Ruth said, ceasing a moment within the silence. "I don't mean just *live*; I mean will he live a real life again? Without the treatments or the drugs or the pain?"

The doctor thought a long moment before answering. "He has a very small chance of that, yes. But without this treatment, Ruth—without having to, unfortunately, experience their painful side effects—he has no chance to live a life worth living at all. Zero." He clicked open a ballpoint pen and slid it across the desk. "Sign the form, guys."

Ruth considered the pen, the two blank lines at the bottom of the page in her hand, and then her husband beside her. His hand reached across the small gap between them and grasped hers with a squeeze.

The SUV's digital speedometer read "10" as the break in the traffic jam reached them. Gerry's right leg trembled from exhaustion and merely moved off and onto the brake, allowing only the pull of gravity to accelerate the vehicle enough to match those proceeding ahead of it.

"I spy something green!" hollered Kandace. To Gerry, the sudden air of innocence was what was most jarring. Or was it naiveté? The others tried to play along with the game they'd started a hundred miles ago.

"Is it bigger than a bread box?" asked Ruth.

"Yes!" replied the little girl with some sense of satisfaction already.

"Duh!" said Lisa with more than a hint of annoyance. "Is it that humongous sign?"

The SUV came alongside the offramp sign that they'd all noticed for over the past half hour. "Exit 9—Rhode Island Coast," it read.

"Hey!" protested Kandace. "It was Daddy's turn to ask! Mommy! Tell her it wasn't her turn!"

While their mother worked to calm the brewing feud in the back, Gerry reached to turn the car's radio back on. A stranger's voice then joined theirs, that of a singular hurried woman, caught mid-sentence.

"—oximately fourteen-hundred hours, thirteen minutes and eleven seconds, Eastern Standard Time. Citizens already outside zone zero are being instructed by military personnel to remain at their present location and seek out the nearest designated shelter. All outgoing roadways reportedly remain fully congested. Vehicle abandonment has been fully authorized. Non-vehicular travel has been permitted on all major roadways. Once again, seek out the nearest shelter to your present location, as indicated on previously distributed maps. At thirteen-hundred hours, seven minutes, eight seconds, this is Harriet Thomas with WNUR, handing off now to Doctor Tobias Hofmann of MIT's Haystack Observatory, with an update on the current position of the Herzog meteor and its expected time of—"

The broadcast was interrupted as Gerry pressed the CD button on the radio. The narration from the audiobook they'd been listening to thirty minutes before broke in.

"—though Hazel guessed that they must now have gone further from the warren than any rabbit he had ever talked to, he was not sure whether they were yet safely away—"

This was the second time they'd heard this part of the story on this ride, though it was from one the girls hadn't yet grown tired of. The comforting voice of the narrator served to somewhat quell the quarreling children; the effect was unintentional, though welcome.

"Listen," Ruth said. "Your father's put the story on again. Just be quiet and be good, please?"

The children sulked and sank back into their seats, the gap between them wider as they pressed against the opposing back doors.

"It's going to be close," Gerry said, just loud enough to reach his wife beside him. "Sounds like another hour to go." He pulled his phone from his shirt pocket and pushed its power on to check the time. One o'clock, ten minutes, fifteen seconds. Telling time was the only thing the phone was good for anymore.

"Thanks for coming, Gerry," Ed Boyd said in a hushed tone. "It means a lot. To Barb too."

The two stood abreast, facing the rows of polished marble slabs adorned with bronze nameplates. Bouquets of flowers occupied vases that hung from crypt doors. Fresh daisies and carnations filled one on the single crypt door they were regarding, and the air was fragrant with them to the point of being overwhelming.

Ed sniffed and raised a hand to his face. Instinctively, Gerry withdrew a handkerchief from his pants pocket and, with it, a shower of coins and lint. The few bits of hitchhiking change fell to the marble floor and interrupted the silence. Gerry caught one with his foot just before it was able to roll too far away.

"God damn—I mean, sorry about that," Gerry said, handing the handkerchief to Ed.

"Oh," Ed said, taking Gerry's offering and applying it to his eyes. "This is mostly allergies, believe it or not. Probably from all these damned flowers. But thanks."

Gerry was momentarily grateful for the short-lived break in the uncomfortable monotony, where talk is solemn, heads are bowed, and hands hang firmly knitted together on laps. He decided keeping that window open with small talk was in his best interest.

"How is she? Barbara. She handle the year okay?"

Ed finished wiping the corners of his eyes and shoved the handkerchief into his suit coat pocket without much thought. "Y'know," he started with a shrug. "She's been able to keep herself busy, keep her mind off things. It got bad again this week, when we got closer to today. It sorta brought up memories again, y'know?"

Gerry did know, indicating as much with only a nod. They both looked toward the mausoleum's entrance and at Ed's wife. The past hour of her heartwarming hugs and smiles came to an end with the closing of the door, the penultimate guest exiting the building. She caught Gerry and Ed's looks and returned a soft smile, looking thoroughly exhausted though relieved that the day had nearly drawn to an end. If not for the toll the past year had taken on the poor woman, she'd have passed as her late daughter's older sister, Gerry thought. It was a thought many had at one time.

"You want to know the truth?" Ed asked. "I think she's more upset these days because of your boy, Gerry."

Gerry turned and gave Ed an incredulous look.

"You know Danny was like a son to us, Gerry," Ed continued. "Like I know Liz was a daughter to you and Ruth. He and Liz were inseparable. We were like a second home to him, and Barb loved that boy like he was one of our own."

Gerry looked away, back again toward the crypt. It was true: Liz had felt like a daughter in some ways. He wondered if Danny still thought of his girlfriend, whether in the brief moments of relief from pain while awake, or within dreams, if they were something his mind was still capable of creating. As if the physical pain was not enough, how would the loss of true love add to the anguish his son had been forced to endure? It was only then that it was a small comfort to know that Danny was, as far as anyone knew, unaware.

Gerry reached in his pants pocket before realizing it was already empty. There were no tears to dry, but there had been solace in knowing the handkerchief was there. Sometimes the mere touch of the cloth in his grasp would serve as a signal to his eyes that it was okay to let the tears fall. Sometimes allowing them to fall felt better, but for Gerry they served only as a short-lived distraction. Ed lay a comforting hand on Gerry's shoulder, as though he'd somehow heard Gerry's internal dialogue.

"How could you say that?" Gerry asked. "I mean, your daughter's... here. My son's alive. How could you feel worse about Danny?"

Ed stood silent a long while before answering, joining Gerry's stare at the words "Elizabeth Boyd" embossed in bronze.

"After the accident, when we heard what happened, and Liz was gone and Danny was in ICU... I won't lie to you, Gerry, we were goddamned pissed off. I think it's one of those things where you want to lash out and blame someone for something like that, and when you've got no one to lash out at, you pick the one who's better off. We heard Danny survived the crash, out cold with his head really bandaged up, but alive. I was so mad, Gerry. *So* mad. I wished it was my Liz in that bed, and Danny was the one who didn't make it."

Ed pulled Gerry's handkerchief back out again for his eyes, less now due to the flower pollen's effects.

"I'm sorry, Gerry," Ed continued. "Like I said, it was a spur-of-the-moment thing, where your mind's all cloudy and you're not thinking straight."

Gerry nodded in understanding.

"But you know what, Gerry? I feel like it's Liz who's better off. Her suffering's done. As far as we know, there wasn't ever any. She was killed instantly. Barb and I, we got over Liz being gone. Well, not really, but we got better about it. Danny, though. Is he getting any better, Gerry?"

"Worse, it seems," Gerry answered. He turned then to face Ed, his tone turning defensive. "He's my boy, Ed. Our son. You think I should wish he was dead? Is that it? That he should be lying in a box right now next to your daughter, rather than alive in that hospital?"

"Danny is suffering, Gerry. We went and saw him, just last week. I don't know why I asked you how he was doing; I saw it for myself. I'm sorry, Gerry, but—" Ed cut himself off, considering for a moment that he may be digging himself a deeper hole. "As much as I miss her, you know as well as I do that Liz probably got the better end of the deal here."

Inside himself, Gerry glared at Ed, and part of him hated Ed for his words. Externally, Gerry remained silent, his eyes dropping to the floor, stopping just beneath Elizabeth's tomb door and at the small pile of offerings of remembrance left there. A delicate figurine of a horse, a few photos and neatly propped-up letters and cards. All of those who'd left them, he knew, remembered the seventeen-year-old girl only as they last saw her alive: happy, radiant, and in love. A larger part of Gerry hated himself for having made decisions that weren't entirely his to make, and for not having had the courage in the first place to do the right thing for Danny.

"—with the risk of finding themselves, in the end, back at the warren—"

Ruth glanced back at their children, now silent and staring out their respective windows. Two more lanes of automobiles lined up to their right, heading in the same direction as they were, moving at the same crawl of a pace. Over the wide grassy median to the left lay the highway's westbound lanes, choked with forsaken cars, busses and trucks, and interspersed with nomadic families on foot. Those carrying children or sacks of belongings on their shoulders advanced much slower than the ones running and unburdened.

Through the closed glass of the sunroof, Gerry made a discreet upward glance to the heavens. The object the world had been fixated on for the past eight days had grown much more visible now in the daytime sky, appearing more like Venus during twilight hours, though this now being nearly mid-day. His eyes welled with tears, more from the pain of a blinding, cloudless sky than of any sadness or joy.

"But what did these sounds mean and where, in this wilderness, could they bolt to?"

For fifty minutes more, they and their surrounding parade rolled at the pace of ants. In that time, Gerry reflected internally. Staring out the windshield at nothing in particular, his wife created her own similar dialogue within.

Their thoughts didn't question whether they were doing the right thing; that was a decision they had made and fully come to terms with several days ago. Reflecting on what was coming was no longer something they had the luxury for. Instead, they filled their minds with what had come before, in times when family trips were to destinations meant for short stays and long-lasting memories. They stole glances at one another from time to time, each with a knowing smile, as they were now far past the feelings of worry and concern.

Gerry's wife grasped his right hand with her left, every now and then giving it a gentle squeeze. It was their own way of saying "I'm thinking of you" without having to say so. Those squeezes, now, came often.

They passed another green sign by the side of the road: 108, Point Judith, 1 Mile.

From the back seat, the sound of paper being unfolded. Into her cross-legged lap, Kandace lay flat the paper on which she had been drawing. Of thin lines in permanent marker was the outline of a small house. From it, a road extending to the opposite side of the paper, terminating at a wide kidney shape of blue, filled with waves formed from lines of interconnecting letter w's. Along the drawn road, a solitary car with four smiling faces. Above the scene shown a beaming sun and, alongside it, a shooting star.

Ignoring her past artwork, the girl turned the paper over. Her markings from the drawn-on side bled through in places among the map already printed there. She traced her finger along a jagged line where blue met brown and green, a thin black coastline where ocean met land. She passed over names of seaside towns unfamiliar to her.

Lisa looked out her window and once again across to the opposing lanes of highway, still blanketed with unmoving automobiles, now with only an occasional glimpse of humanity darting among them. "What's going to happen to all of them?" she asked to anyone who would reply from the front.

"All of who, honey?" her mother asked.

"The people we saw a long time ago, who were going the other way," Lisa clarified. "Are they going to be okay?"

"Those others, many miles back—and the ones before that—they'll have... a difficult life ahead of them, I'm afraid." Ruth stole a concerned peek at her youngest then, who was more absorbed with the map than with the conversation around her.

"What do you mean?" Lisa asked.

Ruth sank back into her seat again and joined her husband's glance up and ahead of them, both fixated upon the same position in the sky at what was previously only visible through the sunroof.

Ruth opened her mouth to speak, hoping to buy herself time while she developed a non-lie answer she could live with.

"Hazel followed; and together they slipped away, running easily down through the wood, where the first primroses were beginning to bloom."

Gerry rounded the corner into Danny's room, carrying two cups of bad hospital coffee, as he heard Ruth read the last line of the book that, as a child, had been their son's favorite. She hadn't heard Gerry enter, though perhaps the smell of coffee or the feeling of another presence in the room cause her to turn her head as she closed the book.

"I've got us some more sludge," Gerry said. "I put a little more creamer and sugar in yours, maybe help it go down easier. I left mine high-test, but I'm not happy about it."

"Oh, no. I'm done, thanks. I've already had enough to keep me up longer than I should, and I have to get up early with the girls."

Gerry had a seat next to Ruth, by Danny's bed, and held onto the silence for a long minute. The scene was unchanged from the countless times they'd been there before, apart from the flowers and cards left recently by visitors marking the date. Gerry fixed on one particular card with the heading of "get well soon," and it struck him as absurd. How much longer is "soon" to get well, when a year had already passed? He took a sip of the coffee meant for him and winced at its bitterness and heat.

"Ed was right," Gerry said softly, more to himself than to Ruth.

"Who? Liz's Ed?" Ruth asked. "What do you mean? Right about what?"

Gerry turned his eyes toward his emaciated and near-lifeless son, who was nearing twenty and looking more like one hundred. "I remember when we got the call, right after the accident. It was Tony, before the police could reach us. He recognized Danny when he was brought in here, though just barely." He took another sip of the high-test as Ruth quietly listened on.

"When we got here... Well, you know. It was bad. We knew Liz was already gone, and Danny was on his way out. Then Tony came to us, let us know what Danny's options were. 'A thousand-to-one shot,' he said. We could sign the forms for the treatment—knowing full well what kind of a ride that meant for our son—or let the flame burn out. Now or never."

"We didn't know for sure what this would do to Danny, Gerry," said Ruth. "We took a chance. For our son. It was that or just let him die."

"But does that mean he's better off? Better off than Liz?"

She didn't answer, only joining her husband's stare at the suffering boy in the bed.

"There'd been times, Ruth, when I thought a thousand-to-one shot was a worthwhile chance to take. The odds were worth it. And now I start to truly wonder if the best shot at success or happiness—or whatever good you want to come out of a situation—is to not take a chance at all."

Kandace's tracing finger fell then on what it'd been searching for. She mouthed the words below the only red dot on the map, bearing the name on the sign they'd just passed: Point Judith. Radiating away from the dot were concentric circles, the innermost also colored red, then yellow, as they grew wider and further from the center.

"They've chosen to make a very risky decision for themselves and their families," Gerry interjected. His right foot hadn't let off the car's brake for the past fifteen minutes, so he shifted into park.

Around them other cars did the same, some occupants opening their doors and stepping outside.

He pushed a button on his cellphone to check the time: two o'clock, eleven minutes, five seconds. He watched for six seconds more, then mentally began to count down from one hundred and twenty. He gave his wife's hand a squeeze.

"The people here, around us. Ahead of us," Ruth added. "We're all making a choice to be certain of our futures. Back there, behind us—where we came from, where those people went—there's a very good chance they'll wind up with a long time of... pain. Suffering. Sadness."

Kandace touched her finger to each circle on the map, starting at the outermost yellow and working inward. To the left and right of each ring, a number, which she read quietly to herself. They reminded her of the magnetic dart board in her playroom back home, where landing a bullseye got one the most points. Odd here, she thought, that this target's points read the other way around.

Inside Gerry's head echoed the number thirty.

"What about us, Mommy?" asked Lisa. "Will we be sad here?"

"No, honey," her mother said. "There's no chance of that."

As Kandace's finger rested on the central dot above Point Judith, she read to herself—as best as she could with her second-grade comprehension—the word written at the top of this odd, targeted map, where the best one could score, dead center, was zero: "survivability."

"Are we there yet?"

"Just a moment more, my love."

Gerry's internal counting reached the number beside the map's singular red dot. His right hand squeezed and did not loosen. The children's book read on, as the world around them filled with a blinding white, not long before the sonic boom reached their ears.

"O take me with you, dropping behind the woods, Far away, to the heart of light, the silence."

MORE CHILLS FROM VELOX BOOKS

MORE CHILLS FROM VELOX BOOKS

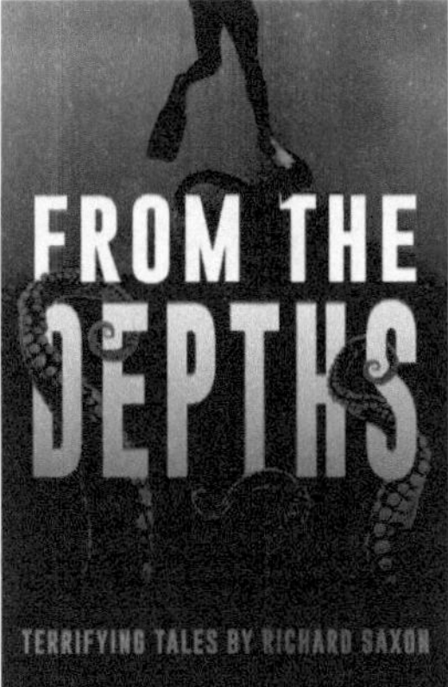

MORE CHILLS FROM VELOX BOOKS

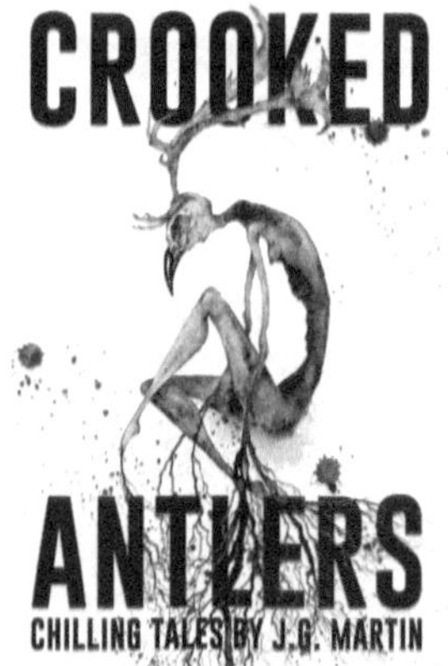